Daddy Didn't

Come Home

Everin Houkom

2017

Daddy Didn't Come Home

Written by

Everin Houkom

The plot line in this story is a true story from my wife's family. Nevertheless, this is a work of fiction. Names, characters, places are either products of the author's imagination or are used fictitiously.

Copyright 2017

Dedicated to my wife Sue and her extended family, whose true-life experiences gave me the backbone of this story.

.

Also dedicated to 4:30 Coffeehouse, where this story was written. Thanks, Tracy, Sheri, Wendy, Anna, and all the others

Part One

Chapter 1

Evening, October 15, 1906

Daddy didn't come home tonight.

Eight year old Billy was ready with his baseball and glove. They always played catch when Daddy came home from his mail route. Some days Daddy would change his clothes out of his mailman uniform but most evenings he just jumped out of the carriage, grabbed his glove from the back, and focused all his attention on Billy.

"Fire that ball in here, son. I'm ready. "

Billy would pitch that ball. Right into his glove. Hard as he could.

"Whoa, where did you get that heat? 'Bout burned a hole in my hand, son. No, no damage done," he would report as he looked at his glove. "Here, fire me another one."

But Daddy didn't come home tonight.

This morning before school, Billy saw Father start off walking, almost running, along the back forest trail to get to town and the mail office. It was a glorious Minnesota October day and Daddy had decided to forgo the horse and buggy to get to work. He was up early and he left the house early. He told Billy that he would be home just after the children got home from school and that Billy should be ready for some baseball as soon as he got home.

Usually Billy walked home from school with his older sister, Johanna. Today, with his first step off the country schoolhouse porch, Billy started running, leaving Johanna far behind. He hadn't stopped racing until he got to the edge of the woods and saw the house before him. He stopped just long enough to catch his breath, bending over his tall, thin body with hands on knees and capturing the fresh farm air in his lungs.

Next he ran up to the front porch, threw his book bundle on the steps and grabbed his baseball glove and tattered baseball off the porch swing. He peeked through the front door into the house to see if Mother had spotted him. With no sign of Mother, he jumped back down to the front yard and headed for the little front gate at the end of the driveway out next to the county road to wait for his father...

Today, Billy had not changed out of his school duds. That was usually one of Mother's rules; change out of your school clothes as soon as you get home. But Mother often looked the other way when she knew Billy and his father were going to play. A boy needed to be with his father as much as possible. Now Billy impatiently waited for what seemed to him like a whole hour, tossing the ball into his glove excitedly. He would flip his scraggly long hair out of the way, and then toss the ball again. Sometimes he threw himself a high pop-up, then he would look for his father again. *I hope Daddy saw me catch that last one.*

Billy ran out to the end of the driveway. Usually Daddy would come up the road from the left. The boy looked long and carefully to the left then shifted his eyes to the right. One time in the spring, Daddy had fooled Billy and doubled back in the woods and appeared from the right. Billy tried to see even a little speck moving on the road up on the far hill but nothing but the leaves moved in the trees.

Suddenly. Billy remembered that Daddy used the path in the woods today. *Of course, I will see him come out of the woods behind the house and then come up the yard past the well.* Billy stared at the entrance to the path. He stared so long his eyes began to see all kinds of things moving there. But no Daddy.

The lad ran back to the front of the house. *I know where he is. I remember that time a month ago when school first started that he was hiding behind the big cottonwood tree and he jumped out and surprised me.* Billy ran around the tree. No surprise today.

Billy took a quick trip out to the old, weathered barn, looking in the stalls and under the hay in the manger and behind the carriage. He looked in the chicken coop. "Daddy, are playing like a chicken today? Cock-a-doodle-do." But no rooster father. The horse whinnied she was hungry. No time for chores now.

Billy had a great idea. I will go around the house and look in each of the windows and doors. Last week Daddy called me from the front door and I couldn't see him in the inner darkness until I was real close. Billy walked around the small shabby white two-story house and peered into each window, moving from side to side to make sure he could see any shadows. Nope, no shadow Daddy.

Billy came back to the front of the house. He was puzzled now, almost worried. He peered down the long driveway again. No father. He squinted once more to see the entrance to the forest path. Nothing.

Billy's mother Ellie stuck her head out the front door of their little house. For just an instance she saw her husband Charles' straw-colored hair out in the yard. No, that haystack of hair was not Charles. That was Billy. Her son had inherited his father's hair color but not his habit to keep it neat and clean. "Charles needs to chop his son's hair down, mow it down to keep it out of his eyes," she noted.

"Supper's almost ready, Billy. Where did your dad run off to?"

"He didn't come home yet, Mom. He promised he would be early today and he's not here."

Mom moved out to the edge of the porch and looked down the driveway, stretching her neck to see down the distant county road. The sun was already falling out of the western sky as dusk approached.

Her thoughts were racing, "Where could Charles be? He didn't have any plans tonight, not that he told me. He told me this morning he wasn't going to waste any of this afternoon sunshine. Today was made for baseball, he had proclaimed."

"Well, we can wait another five minutes but then we will have to eat our supper before it gets cold. And you need to get your homework finished. Teacher sent that note yesterday saying your last spelling test was not your best."

The door creaked open and little Mary came out the door. "Mommy, I'm hungry. When is supper?" Ellie petted her four-year-old head and scooted her back into the kitchen. "Supper is almost ready, honey. Will you help me set the table?"

"Mommy, we always have supper before the sun hides behind the trees."

Johanna, her sixteen year old daughter had all her school books sprawled out on the far end of the table. She had begun her homework as soon as she had come in the door from school. There was no room in the little house for a desk or study area. Dinner would be set up at the other end of the oak table. Now Ellie took a long look at her grown-up daughter. She was so pretty sitting there with her long, silky hair and her hand-carved necklace around her long neck. "Jo, did Father tell you anything about being late today?"

"No, Mother. He yelled over his shoulder as he ran out the door that he would be home early enough to play lots of silly baseball with Billy. I hope he gets home in time to help me with my latest math lessons."

After Ellie gave the forks and spoons to Mary to distribute she went out on the front porch. She rubber-necked another look down the road. "Where is he?" she said to herself, a little worry creeping into her voice. She sat down on the porch swing, let it sway maybe two times only, and then sprang up again. "Where are you, Charles? This is not funny! You need to get home now!"

Chapter 2

Ellie was confused about her husband's absence. Charles always finished his mail route soon enough to get home for supper. Charles thoroughly enjoyed his postal job. He had told Ellie that the route was sufficiently long to ensure he would be needed at the post office job but left plenty of time for Charles to gab and solve the problems of this world with his neighbors along the way. He usually liked to walk some of the route but would keep his eyes on the time and use his post office buggy if he was running late. But he had never, in the last 3 years, been late for supper without letting Ellie know.

Usually Charles took the family buggy into town to work. The Stadler home was about four miles out northwest of town. That was if one took the regular road. At the edge of town, the road dove down south along the river until it got to the one lone bridge crossing, about two miles, then headed northwest up in the direction of their homestead. Charles could cut off a big chunk of that time though by hiking the forest path starting out behind the yard and crossing the river in the woods. He had discovered this route two summers ago. A large log had fallen across the river from one high bank to the other. A careful person could shimmy that log across the river in no time. That saved the brave soul over three miles and many precious minutes.

The weather was good today, blue sky with those wispy summer clouds floating high in the sky. No storms for the past four days--no muddy roads. Nothing to hold Charles up. Maybe he had gotten into one of those long, heated political discussions with George Martin or Hans Hanson. But if he was going to be real late he would have called the neighbors and they would have relayed the message to Ellie. The Stadlers didn't have a phone at their house. But Charles would not want to worry her. He was very considerate that way; he never wanted to worry her.

The first couple years that Charles worked at the post office he had stopped off at the tavern once in awhile after work. But the last time that had happened was more than three years ago. He had followed Clarence Jamieson into the Muddy Water Pub that evening. He forgot to call. Finally, Ellie ended up collecting all the children, even baby Mary, and driving the carriage into town by the light of the moon and stars. She found him almost asleep, sitting at the bar with three other groggy friends. Charles was so embarrassed when he saw Ellie and the children come into the tavern that he came staggering right out of that pub with his tail between his legs and all the way home he begged Ellie's forgiveness. All the way home he vowed he would never do that again. Ellie smiled to herself. To this day he had kept his word.

But now it was almost dark and there was no sign of Charles. The sun was low in the west and Billy was still out in the yard waiting for Daddy, baseball glove in hand. Billy loved the time he got with Charles to throw the ball back and forth. It was always great bonding time. Usually a life lesson would be thrown into the game as the ball whipped back and forth. Without any trouble at all, as the ball whistled between them, Charles could get Billy to talk about his school lessons or the playground bullying or the importance of school. Things that a mother could not drag out of her son even with a cookie bribe or a piece of pie.

Mary, their little 4 year old princess, was in love with her Daddy, too. She worshiped the ground he walked across. She loved to dress up in her frilliest dress and wait for Charles to dote on her. Tonight she had been absorbed in her dollhouse and little wooden people and animals that lived in those tiny dollhouse rooms. Nonetheless, it hadn't taken long before she noticed her dad's absence. Now she was lining up the silverware by each plate, one fork and one spoon for each person. Ellie withheld the sharp knives in a pile on the counter. She would put them out next to the plates just before serving supper. Mary had asked where her father was at least three times already.

Ellie stirred the beef stew on the burner, not wanting the

chunks of vegetables to stick on the bottom. The smell of fresh-baked bread wafted through the kitchen. Usually a very pleasing smell, today it brought a wave of nausea to Ellie. She fought back the feeling in her stomach, then patted the slight bulge in her lower abdomen and smiled. Charles doesn't know about this little one yet. Tonight, after supper, I will tell him the news. He will be excited, but worried. Worried that we have barely enough room in the house now for the five of us. Worried about another mouth to feed. But excited to bring another baby into God's kingdom.

Ellie waited another five minutes, closer to ten. She dished up the stew and cut a few pieces of the fresh bread for the children. Then she called her son in to supper. Billy did not want to come in from the yard without his father. She had to coax him and coax him.

Billy finally came to the table, carrying his glove and ball with him. "Put the glove down on the floor, Billy. Your stew is getting cold."

"I want to be ready when Daddy comes home so we can play catch right away. Daddy always wants to play before he eats his supper."

"Maybe not tonight, son. The sun is about to set and the light will be gone soon. Come on, now. Eat your supper. Don't you want to have some of my fresh bread?"

Billy placed his baseball glove and ball right next to his plate.

His mother noticed it there but did not comment again. He poked at the food with his fork, moving it from one side of the plate to the other. Ellie did get him to eat about half his usual portion of stew and half a piece of buttered bread.

His two sisters were quite the opposite, hustling up to the table and sticking their chins right down by the stew and slurping it in spoonful after spoonful. "Mind your manners, young ladies. Just because Father is not here does not mean you can eat like lumberjacks."

Ellie tried to eat some stew as well. She picked at the potatoes and carrots and a couple smaller pieces of the beef. "That's enough for this stomach tonight," she thought. "I will munch on a dry slice of bread while I clean up the dishes."

She talked with herself as she cleared up the table. "I know this feeling will be gone in a few more weeks but I am so miserable. I suppose it doesn't help that Charles is late. I have always been a worrier. He will show up. And he will have a good reason for his tardiness. I just wish we had a telephone now. It's too late to run over to the Schultz' house at this hour. I must get the children to their home studies and then up to bed. School time will come early tomorrow."

She cleared the table, insisting Billy stay right there in his chair until she was done. Then Ellie sat with him at the table and practiced his list of spelling words with him. He didn't pay much attention to the lesson. After reviewing the list three times, she sighed to herself and hustled Billy off upstairs. He never did spell "thought" correctly.

Billy climbed upstairs, changed into his warm pajamas, leaving his socks on for warmth, and said his prayers. "And an extra prayer for Daddy, too. God, keep Daddy safe, wherever he is."

It took an extra long while for Billy to fall asleep. The sky had turned pitch black by the time he got real sleepy. The last thought in his head was Daddy didn't come home tonight.

Mary had completely depleted her energy level by the time supper was done. A minor whine session came when she was hustled up to bed and she realized Daddy wasn't there to read her bedtime story. But after only two pages of her sister Johanna's reading Mary was in dreamland.

Johanna completed her home assignments at the kitchen table. She could see how worried her mother was about Father's absence. It made her uneasy also, but she reasoned that her father was a grown-up and could take care of himself. He was a smart man. He'll explain everything to us tomorrow.

"Good night, Mother. Please greet Father for me when he comes home."

Now, sitting at the kitchen table alone, Ellie was confused. But more than that, she was worried. Where is that man?

Chapter 3

Morning, October 15

Charles loved the early morning air on these October days. He closed his mouth and took a deep breath through his nose. It tickled, felt cool and refreshing, as it tracked down his throat. He loved the cleansing crispness in his nose and sinus passages. His lungs were washed by the pure life-giving oxygen.

'This is a great morning to walk to work. I will trek through the woods on the short cut path into town, then head into the mail office. That will warm up my legs. Then when I am finished with my route this afternoon I can skedaddle home to have a little extra time with Billy before supper. He loves to throw the baseball back and forth. I do too. Quality time.'

Mostly Charles ran on the forest path, jumping over the fallen branches. Most of this trail traveled in the wooded terrain at the ends of the farmers' lots. He lingered once at the crest of the third hill to crane his neck toward the east and see the big lake on the horizon, past the forest. He paused again to inspect a ring of wild mushrooms that had sprung up since his last time through the woods. He traversed the log bridge across the river, scooting slowly and carefully on his seat on the wet bark. That was the only obstacle that slowed him down. Overall he made great time.

As he approached the short, squat little building that housed the postal service he noted how quiet it looked. No buggies in the street; no lights on in the building.

"I beat Ralph in today. That will give me a little more room on the long counter so I can sort the mail more quickly. This is shaping up to be a great day all around," he thought outloud.

Once inside the office, he set to work immediately. The stuffed mail bag was sitting just inside the back door. It had been dropped off in the middle of the night, all the mail from the Alexandria office. The bag's quite heavy today. Good thing I came early this morning, he thought.

His hands worked quickly and efficiently, sorting out the letters and packages for Ralph and himself; he placed Ralph's stack over on the other end of the bench. While sorting, he divided his own mail into orderly piles for the various neighbors that he would visit later on the route.

I wonder if Mrs. Nelson is feeling better now. Her pneumonia had taken a long time to disappear. She had been so weak that he had to walk up right onto her porch and wait patiently for her to reach the front door. He had noticed that the last two days she had opened that door more quickly and appeared less short of breath. Yep, here are two letters from her out-of-state cousins. Her mail had increased a lot with her illness; everyone who couldn't be here in Centerville wanted to help keep her spirits up.

Ralph arrived at his usual time, surprised to see that Charles had done so much already. Charles moved his stacks of mail further over to his half of the bench, keeping them carefully in order.

"Hi, Ralph. You sleep in today? Up playing cards last night?"

"I'm here at my usual time, young man. Who shot you out of a cannon today?"

"Oh, I just woke up to the birdsong in the yard and watched the sun come up. What an inspiring morning! I am hoping to get home early today so I can enjoy a little more time with my son Billy and my daughters Mary and Johanna. Before long the days will be shorter and the winter darkness will descend. We have a lot of outdoor things to do before then."

"I know what you mean, Charles. When I was your age I did the same thing. Now I treasure the little extra time in the morning to get my joints moving. Sometimes I wish I could take an oil can to them."

"Oh, you move pretty well for all your years. I hope to be as spry as you when I'm at that age."

"I hide a lot of the pain, young man. I hide a lot of the pain."

Just then, he dropped a couple letters on the floor and bent slowly to pick them up.

"Hear that squeaking in my knees? That's just what I mean."

Charles just laughed. He had continued working on his

sorting during this conversation. The last letter, and his one and only package, went into the Nelson pile. Now he arranged them all in his bag just right. He was ready. Looking at his watch he saw that he was 35 minutes early on his start.

Hope that old horse is ready to go early, Charles thought to himself. Sometimes Old Grey is just as slow to get moving as Ralph claims to be. I wonder if those clever doctors are developing anything for Ralph's creaking joints. What a gold mine that would be!

Loading up the buggy went quickly. Charles was right though about the horse. That critter just stood at the hay bale and munched contentedly. Charles knew what to do. He had a stash of his juicy garden carrots in the bag in the corner and as soon as the mare saw the orange color in Charles' hands she was animated and ready to go. "Here you are, Old Grey! Let's go."

It was 8:45 when he left the post office. "This is a great start to a great day! God is good!" he proclaimed to the empty street.

He headed out of town on West Road. His route took six hours to complete, twenty miles of country roads. No sense trying to rush Old Grey out there in the country. That horse enjoyed the solitude as much as he did.

The rising sun felt warm on his neck. He loved the clear blue sky dotted with little wispy clouds. What a perfect day!

Chapter 4

Charles slowly headed out of the city limits, past the row of old dilapidated mansions on Main Street, and out past the new church just erected at the edge of the woods. The pastor's buggy was already parked there next to the church. The black horse was contentedly chewing on her morning hay. That young reverend is really dedicated to his parish; always here studying the Scripture or out visiting his parishioners. Good to have that young man move into the town. Reverend Jorstad from Pennsylvania. Good to have a voice that was not echoing all the Scandinavian voices here in the county. Thinks for himself, talks for God.

Charles grabbed the bundle of church mail and entered the side door. He peered into the office but it was empty. Pastor must be in the sanctuary, maybe with a parishioner. I'll see him tomorrow.

About two miles out of town and ten stops along his route, he pulled up to front edge of the Hanson homestead, a nice big home with plenty of pasture and fields to support a big, Midwestern family. Unfortunately, Hans and Edith had had only two children. Emil was a bachelor son still living at home. Hans junior had run off to Alaska country, chasing the gold rush and the fast life. The Hansons hadn't heard from him since his first letter three years ago asking for a big stack of money to invest in a sure-thing gold strike. Not surprising when Hans's letter back told his son in no uncertain terms to never bring that subject up again.

Charles had walked by the back side of this place this morning while on the path on the way into work. Now, in the distance, he could hear that Hans and son Emil were already back there working on the new well. They had been at it for several days, digging the deep hole and fortifying the walls with stones and brick. The old well was going dry; it might not last past the end of autumn. Well-digging was hard work but water was essential. Charles hoped they had some help coming today. He could help on Saturday, if they were still digging. He waved cordially but he could not get their attention now as he drove up along the road in front of the property. The men were way in the far back of the lot. Charles only saw one man by the tall pile of dirt. The other worker must have been down in the well shaft.

Charles pulled up at the front of the house. Having seen the buggy turning the corner down by the abandoned Jones farm, Edith was already walking out to meet him at the end of the foot path. Edith always had a big smile on her face. She looked like she had an everlasting secret on her mind or was planning the biggest practical joke. She was just filled with her love of God and His constant presence.

"Hello, Charles. Got much mail for us today."

"Couple letters here. Nothing from young Hans, though. Would sure be good to hear from him and know he is safe."

"You are right there. But I am sure he is still scared off by that letter he got from his father. I imagine the paper was still smoking when it arrived in Alaska from the fiery words Hans wrote."

"Maybe your husband's letter burned up on the way! Boy, I never heard of fire hazard in my postal job before! "

"Oh, Charles. You are so comical. Thanks for your service."

"Always a pleasure, Edith. Always a pleasure. Tell Hans I can help on Saturday if the well is not finished."

"They will probably be done tonight or early in the morning. Those two have been working like the devil out there. It's making them pretty ornery too. I will be very glad when that project is done."

The rest of the route wandered by as Charles stopped at each house. Everybody had at least one piece of mail in the bag today. That was unusual for this route. Some of those old bachelor farmers and aging widows could go a week or two without anything. He hoped each piece of mail brought happiness on this great sunny day.

He did stop longer at Mrs. Nelson's place. He walked up the path, bypassing the mailbox, knocked on the door and waited. Behind the door he could hear the scurrying of her walk in the front room.

That sounded more like her usual speed. She must be recovering nicely now from that nasty pneumonia.

"Hello, Mrs. Nelson. You are one lucky lady. I think you got half the mail in my bag today. Look at all these letters. And a package to boot. "

"Oh, goodness. All my shirt-tail relatives been coming out of the woodwork since I turned sick." She looked back into her humble house and laughed. "Must be lining up to inherit this royal palace!"

"You have a beautiful little home here, Mrs. Nelson. I can see all the love you have put into this place. And it's just right for you, just right for you."

The gray mare slowed down a couple times along the way, munching on the patches of fresh grass. Charles let her graze. No need to hurry now. Just soak up the wonderful sunshine. I am still running ahead today. I can still enjoy the extra time with the children this afternoon.

As he rode back into the edge of town he pulled out his trusty pocket watch. Three o'clock on the button. Good, I should be able to get home before four today.

He pulled up behind the mail office, took care of the horse and buggy and walked in the front door. No one is back yet, he thought. Ralph won't be back for another hour at least. The city routes, much longer and busy, often lasted until six.

He went to the back bench to put his bag away. There on the bench was a package, a package he had missed in the morning.

"In my rush this morning, I must have mistakenly put that one in Ralph's pile. Oh, silly me. No harm done. I can drop it off as I run home.

Chapter 5

Evening

Supper was finished and Charles still wasn't home. He had been late like this so seldom that Ellie could count on one hand the times. And with all the other times he had always let her know somehow. They had given up their telephone in the house about 3 years ago. They just couldn't afford it on their meager budget. The Schultz family that lived down the road would occasionally run over with a message for them. Edward Schultz was the one that had told Ellie the bad news about her father when he had his horrible accident back home in Ohio. It was so hard for Mr. Schultz to bring out the words as Ellie stood in front of him with a look that matched his mournful face. She knew something was terribly wrong. She rarely got phone messages. That Ed Schultz was a good friend and neighbor. And Gert Schultz was wonderful those first weeks after father's death, too. Both Ellie and Charles were from Ohio. Ellie had no family support here. Sometimes she wondered why they had been so keen on moving out here to Minnesota. Her mother had passed away while giving birth to a stillborn son seven years after Ellie was born. He would have been Ellie's only sibling.

Ellie had always been a loner growing up. Without her mother around, her aunts and neighbor ladies had kept an eye on her. Her father was a hard worker in the factory, putting in long double shift days to make ends meet at home. When he got home, he was exhausted and thus there wasn't much conversation around. Ellie knew he did his best to raise her but watched her friends and their families and knew she was missing a lot at home. Once in a while her best friend Julie would invite her to go skating or to attend her church.

Charles, on the other hand, was a talker. Boy, could he talk. She was drawn to him immediately because he was so different from her father. She loved the attention Charles paid to her. They courted for a short time and then Charles boldly asked Ellie's father for her hand in marriage. Father liked Charles also. He had never had a son and welcomed the companionship. He also recognized the love that Charles showed to Ellie. The wedding was simple but glorious. Of course there were some bittersweet tears with the absence of her mother, but a beautiful celebration nonetheless.

One month after the wedding, Charles proposed that they move west. Starting a new life together from scratch felt exciting and she agreed to the plan. Father had done nothing but support the idea wholeheartedly. He figured he would enjoy traveling out to see them; it would be an adventure for him too. In fact, he mentioned more than once that he might want to settle near them later, especially when all the wonderful grandchildren began to arrive.

Ellie realized that she was only a year older than Johanna was now when they packed up one suitcase each and hopped into her father's buggy for the long ride to the train station. The young couple was filled with optimism and great plans. Sitting next to her new husband on the train had felt so good as they held hands and hugged at every stop. The only plan they had was to settle in Minnesota. Charles had a friend who had moved there the year before and had written Charles about the many opportunities available. They jumped off in Centerville when Ellie spied the tranquil lake in the distance as the engine slowed to a stop at the station. This town looked too good to pass up.

Those first years in Minnesota had unfortunately been very lonely. Charles' friend had moved on further west by the time they arrived in Minnesota. They knew no one at all in the town of Centerville. Everything was so different here in Minnesota compared to Ohio. Charles found a job easily at a livery stable, mostly repairing the saddles and equipment. Ellie cleaned house for some of the older matriarchs in town. Each mansion took a whole day to clean; there was no shortage of work for her. Money always seemed to run out a day or two before Charles' payday, however.

What a surprise when Ellie discovered she was pregnant. She had a nice cluster of friends among the other cleaners and maids in the town. She got lots of advice and plenty of used baby clothes. Late pregnancy was a challenge because Ellie had to stop her work once the baby was big enough to show. Her employers would not allow an expectant mother to do any manual labor, especially with her first child. Luckily, the labor and delivery had flowed much more smoothly than she had imagined. To see that beautiful baby girl Johanna---Ellie named her after her mother--- wrapped up in the blankets was her greatest joy yet. She was totally surprised when, a few days later, she crashed deep into the pit of depression.

Breastfeeding was not going well; her milk supply was marginal. The baby cried constantly. Nothing seemed to console Johanna. Charles would come home tired from work and find both Ellie and Johanna crying. He was lost as to how to help them. Maybe the worst part of this was that Ellie missed her mother. She needed her mother now. Really needed her. Mother would have known exactly what to do and how to console Ellie. Mothers always knew just what to do. But Mother was gone. When Ellie's father came to visit she felt even worse because the absence of her mother was even more real. How did the new family survive this time? With patience and love and lots of tense crying sessions.

Charles had been no more prepared for family life than she had been. By the second month, he began to stop off at the pub after work for a quick beer. He would lose track of time, crawling home to her asking forgiveness. He needed his friends. She knew that. He needed the joking and talk bantered between the young coworkers at the pub. But she needed him too. She needed him at home. Once the baby colic settled and Ellie learned how to care for Johanna and her little idiosyncrasies, family life began to calm down and Charles didn't need the pub time as much. That was a great period.

Excitement built up again about three years later when Ellie felt the tell-tale signs of another baby. Charles so hoped for a son. Then one day about two months later Ellie started bleeding and cramping vigorously and she knew she had lost the baby. This round of depression was so much deeper than with Johanna. Charles' dashed hopes for Charles Junior hit him just as hard. As is so often true, the demands of little three year old Johanna kept the young couple grounded and gradually home life returned to a peaceful pace.

No sooner had the couple scratched their way out of the hell they were in than Ellie had a second failed pregnancy, another miscarriage. This time the postpartum period was so devastating that Charles totally unraveled and ended up disappearing for a few weeks. Ellie thought he went west somewhere, Montana or Colorado, maybe. Charles never told her where he went. What he did tell her when he came home was that he had learned out on the road that he could never be without her or Johanna again. He also proclaimed that he was done with the taverns and drinking. He realized that they only put him in a bad state, thinking about himself and not about his family. That epiphany was ten years ago now.

Charles got his son eight years ago. Billy was perfect. Just perfect-- and at the perfect time. Charles would now have someone to share the outdoors with, someone to teach all the manly things he had in his head. As he grew up, Billy adored his father. He followed him everywhere and imitated him as much as he could.

Lately, her son's obsession was baseball. Billy was rarely separated from his little glove and ball. Ellie wasn't sure who got more pleasure from this sport, her little-kid husband or her grown-up son. It was so fun to watch the two of them throwing the ball back and forth. Charles was doing such a good job of raising their son.

.   But now there was no sign of Charles. Ellie reviewed what she knew. She knew that he had walked into work today. Their horse Blackie and buggy were in the barn and she and Mary had taken the horse out to the pasture to exercise during lunch time. She remembered her pleasure sitting out on the picnic blanket. The sun was good for both human and horse. Blackie did not want to come back in from the field. Ellie and Mary didn't either. Actually, Charles had undoubtedly run to work this morning. He loved to run in the early morning air. He had a nice trail he followed through the woods which ran along the banks of the river. He had to cross over the river on the big log that had fallen over the water last year. He had described the crossing and the loud noises of the rushing water to her. She now winced at that picture in her mind but Charles had assured her that the crossing was safe. "I'll be careful, honey, you know that. You know that."

"I hope you were careful, husband."

Chapter 6

Evening

While working at her home studies at the table, Johanna finally began to feel the anxiety that her mother felt. Evenings after supper was always when she and Father sat at the table and worked on her school work together. It was a special time, a time when she had Father all to herself. Even with the bustle of her mother and siblings around them, they were lost in their own world.

Johanna was 16 now and was a very good, hard-working student. She took great pride in her work and in her status at the head of her class. This was her final year in the rural school. She had started planning already for post-graduation. She wanted to attend the University in Minneapolis. She had dreamed of this since her college-educated teacher arrived five years ago. She did not yet know what field of study she would pursue. Teaching and nursing were usually the only fields open to young women, but she might just upset the apple cart and try something like engineering. Math was so interesting to her. Actually, it was her passion. The way all the calculations fit together in an orderly fashion was amazing. She liked order in her life. Order was good. Father had kept telling her that the freedom this country gave a person allowed that person to dream anything. Absolutely anything, he said. Johanna could dream--no, actually see---herself as anything she wanted, even a mathematician. And now to prove that very point, the University was offering a special proficiency test in math this fall to help find young enrollees like her. What a chance! The university had mailed the exam right here to Centerville to her teacher. The test was tomorrow. Freedom was great--and dreams were great, too.

That was why she began to feel worried about her father's absence. He was part of the central order in her personal life. He could be counted on each evening to be home for supper. Every evening. Each night at the supper table he led off with all the interesting news he had learned from the people on his mail route. Then he would ask the children about each one's day. And he listened carefully to their responses. His questions always showed he had been listening to them. Even the simplest things: like the butterfly Mary saw in the front yard, the game of tag that Billy played at lunch break, the poem Jo had recited in English class. Later, sitting alone at the table, the complex math problems Johanna would discuss were valuable to him as well. She knew that he didn't understand the math but he knew and felt the importance the problems and solutions held in Johanna's mind. He shared her dreams about college. Secretly they had talked about her goals. He had pointed out the extra difficulty that Johanna would have in entering such a far away school and the difficulties trying to obtain a place in the math program there as a young woman. But never once did he tell her it was out of her reach. Never once did he tell her to lower her sights. And never once did either of them mention these things with Mother. Oh, goodness, no way. Her maternal anxieties would overwhelm her.

But tonight Father was not in his chair at the supper table. He was not there to talk about the school day. She wanted to tell him about the trigonometry problems she had solved in math today. In the country school she alone worked on these advanced topics. Johanna realized that Miss Block didn't even know this material. Tonight, without Father, she felt as alone in her homework as she had ever felt. Where is Father? I want to talk to him one more time about the strategy for the test tomorrow. I need him here.

She glanced over at Mother at the sink, cleaning the dishes from supper. Mother's shoulders were slumped over; she was leaning her weight on the front of the sink. She looked so tired tonight. Her spark was gone. She wasn't behaving in her usual way, chasing the children to their homework corners by the hearth or scooting them upstairs to prepare for bedtime.

Johanna also knew that lately her mother was having trouble with her stomach. Over the past few days she was hardly eating anything. Even her favorite meals were left on her plate, picked over but not eaten. Hope she is alright. Maybe mother should go see the doctor in town.

Johanna's homework took longer than usual tonight. Father did not help her directly with her math but his attention always kept her attention focused. The solutions did not roll out as easily tonight. When she closed her books she glanced at the clock in the front room. Oh, my goodness, I need to get these children to bed. I will let Mother rest this evening.

"Come on, children. Time for baths and story time and pajamas and into bed. Let's go upstairs. "

After some weak token protests, and one more look out the window and down the road, Billy and Mary dragged themselves up the stairs. Billy still had his old baseball glove on his hand.

Chapter 7

Night

Pitch black filled the windows. Ellie was now overwhelmed with worry about Charles. Something terrible must have happened to him. Something dreadful. She felt her whole being shaking. Her hands betrayed the tremors. She reached up to remove her glasses so she could clean the tears. She could not grab them. The shakiness was too strong. She left them on her nose; she did not want them all twisted up because of her clumsiness.

What happened to him? Was he attacked by a wolf along the path in the woods? She had heard Charles talk about a man in the next town that had been circled by a pack of wolves last month and the severe injuries he had sustained. He had barely lived through the ordeal. Luckily someone came by the man early enough so that the doctor had a chance to patch him up before he lost too much blood. What if Charles was lying in the woods alone? No one else used that forest path any more. He could just be lying there bleeding to death. She closed her eyes tightly around that bloody image. Then she suddenly pictured the log bridge over the river. What if he had one of his dizzy spells when crossing that log? He had told her that twice this summer he had gotten very lightheaded out in the barnyard on a busy day. He had staggered into the house and devoured slices of buttered bread until he felt better. The stubborn man had wanted no part with consulting the doctor. He was in such a blessed hurry this morning. What if he had skipped lunch to save more time today?

Ellie stoked the fire for the night and lay down on the couch in the front room to wait for Charles. "I won't be able to fall asleep until he gets home, but I can rest," she confided to the walls.

Chapter 8

The next morning

As the dawn sun filtered in through his bedroom window, Billy began to come to his morning awareness. His eyes still not open, he smelled leather. His fingers felt his baseball glove lying on the pillow next to his ear. Now he felt the baseball pressing in under his left shoulder. Why are these in bed with me? Then he remembered that he had gone to bed without seeing Daddy last night.

Daddy will have some explaining to do when I see him this morning. He missed our throwing practice last night. He missed supper, too. Maybe he had to help someone last night; maybe an emergency. Billy threw off the covers and grabbed his ball and glove. His bare feet hit the cold floorboards, but off he went--no time for socks this morning.

He ran down the hall past his sisters' room and into his parent's room. "Daddy, Daddy! Wake up!"

The room was empty. Both Mommy and Daddy were gone. Downstairs already? He ran down the hall to the stairs and headed down to the kitchen.

His sisters stirred in their room when they heard the thundering sounds of their little brother going down the steps. Johanna unfolded herself from the down comforter, nestling her little sister back to sleep quietly in the bed they shared.

Jo followed her brother down the stairs, after noting for herself that the big bed in her parents' room was empty-- and untouched.

The two children stopped at the bottom of the staircase. A loud snoring was coming from the couch. Peering over the back of the couch, they saw mother's hair sticking up unnaturally above her head and her arm contorted out in the air like a big twisted branch of an oak tree. Oh, Mother, you look so funny. Then the same thought hit them both simultaneously.

This is Mother. But where is Father?

Instinctively Ellie felt her children's presence above her. She began to awake, not sure where she was. The soft light of dawn from the window pulled her out of sleep. She saw the fireplace in front of her and recognized the front room. She had been there on the couch all night; Charles had not come home. She straightened up on the couch, running her hands through her tangled hair. Charles did not come home! she thought.

The children ran around the end of mother's makeshift bed and grabbed and hugged her as she stood. The three grasped each other tightly for several seconds then collapsed together on the cushions behind them.

"Where's Daddy! Mom, he didn't come home last night."

"I know, Billy. I just don't understand either. Why are you awake so early?"

"I saw the sun coming up in my window and remembered that Daddy and I did not play any catch yet. We always play catch."

Johanna gave Billy an extra big hug, took the ball from him and tossed it gently toward his gloved hand. Billy caught the ball, almost, but let it fall through his glove netting and let it roll up his arm and onto the floor. Tears appeared at the corners of his eyes and once again he hugged his mother tightly as reality of his father's absence took hold.

Ellie was wide awake now as well. "Johanna, you must take the buggy into town right away and find the sheriff. We must look for your father. He didn't come home. He might be in danger." She couldn't erase the vivid dreams about the wolves and the log bridge.

"But Mother I need to be in school today for a big important math test. This test is like an entrance test for college. I can't miss it! "

"Your teacher will understand when she hears your father is missing. You are a good student. No, let me rephrase that. You are the best student in class. Miss Block will understand. We must find Father and I cannot leave the children alone here at the house. Now please go get dressed quickly and drive into Centerville."

Johanna was not pleased. Her worry about her father was now doubled with her worry about the math test. She could not picture her life without either one. But the look on her mother's face told her she had no choice. She started to stamp up the stairs to change her clothes. Halfway up, she turned back to make eye contact with Mother and gave her a nod of understanding. The teenager ran back down to look her mother straight on, eye to eye. "Of course I will go into town. We are talking about Father."

"Can I go with Johanna?" Billy chirped. "Can I go? I can help."

"No, son, you must stay here with Mary and me at the house. You are the man of the house now this morning. You need to feed the animals and help start the stove for me. You are my big boy today, my big boy!"

Ellie knew that she would need to keep Billy busy today, keep his mind off his father.

All three stood in a huddle. "We need to get through today! Charles is safe, I know he is. He has to be! He has to be safe!"

Chapter 9

Johanna raced up the stairs, slamming her bedroom door shut in her haste. Little Mary squirmed in her bed.

"I am sorry I was so loud, Mary. I need to drive into town right away. You go back to sleep."

The gravity of the moment began to penetrate her anger, pushing her test aside. Usually very careful about her appearance, this morning Johanna just threw on a sundress and a sweater. "My father is missing. What am I thinking? Of course, I will ride into town quickly. I'll probably still have time to get to the schoolhouse before mid-morning. I can still take that math test this afternoon."

She ran down the stairs and headed for the barn. The horse was sleepily poking around the hay trough, not fully awake.

"Come on, Blackie. We have a little trip this morning." Hooking up the buggy was easy and in two minutes Johanna was opening the barn door and driving off to the road that led to town.

The morning sun was now peeking above the trees but the road was still treacherous because of the rocks embedded in the gravel.

Blackie swerved around some of the bigger ones herself but Johanna's attention was definitely on the road to help the horse.

That attentiveness pushed the worries about her father below the surface. Before she realized it, she was crossing the river bridge. The clap clap clap of Bessie's hoofs on the wood planks jolted her mind back to her primary task. After crossing the bridge the road into town was much better, having been improved years ago by the town fathers to promote their interests on Main Street. In a couple more minutes she was driving up to the sheriff's office, tying up her rig, and entering the front door to the jailhouse.

"Johanna, young lady, what in the world brings such a fine young filly like you into the jailhouse so early in the morning. I just arrived myself. The coffee is still brewing in the back room." She looked across the big oak desk to see Sheriff Braun rising from his chair.

"Sheriff, father never came home last night. He has never not come home. Something dreadful has happened to him. We must look for him right now. Something dreadful has happened. I just know it."

"Now, now. Calm down, Johanna. Take a big breath. Slow down and tell me everything you know about this. I'm sure your father is fine. He's just fine." He pulled a chair out from the desk for Johanna to sit down.

"Father didn't come home last night and didn't come home this morning and..." She broke down in sobs, covering her eyes and nose with her hands.

Sheriff Braun gave her his hankie and waited a moment. "Okay, please tell me again, from the very beginning."

"Mother says Father left for work yesterday a bit early and headed down the back pathway, walking and jogging into the woods. He likes to take the shortcut on a nice day and she knew that he wanted to get home early so he could spend more time after school with Billy and Mary and me. In the afternoon, he would have run back the same way. But Billy never saw him coming. Billy had his glove and ball all ready but Father never came. We waited dinner as long as we could. Mother waited up and fell asleep on the couch. Billy got up first this morning and Father was still not home. Something dreadful has happened, Sheriff."

Sheriff Braun began to feel the impact of this report. Charles always thought of his family first. He must have tried to let Ellie know where he was.

"Didn't you get a call on the phone, Johanna?"

"Sheriff, we don't have a phone in the house any more. Father decided we could not afford such a luxury. Sometimes Mr. Schultz comes over with a message for us, but he didn't come last night. We haven't heard a thing."

Johanna blew her nose and wiped her face. "Oh, I am sorry. Look what I did with your hankie. "

"That's alright. I got a whole drawer of those things. Listen, Johanna. I will look into this as soon as Deputy Coffey comes in the door. He should be here before the hour. You run on home and tell your mother I will investigate. We will find him."

He didn't say," Don't worry" because he was beginning to have a great deal of worry himself. He saw her to the door and watched her climb up the buggy and drive back out of town.

"This is strange," Sheriff Braun spoke out loud. "Charles didn't go home last night. What could be going on here? What could be going on?"

Chapter 10

Johanna had much less trouble getting home. The rising sun exposed the rocks and ruts in the road. And she was thinking more clearly now. Talking with the sheriff had helped immensely. Sheriff Braun was Father's friend and he would find Father. She just knew it.

Johanna realized about half the way home that she had only pulled her brush through her hair a couple times before she left for town. She had chosen an old worn dress and her sweater did not match color at all. Jo was usually a very fastidious dresser and her hair normally had a sheen and silkiness from at least a hundred brush strokes. What did the Sheriff think of her this morning? But then she came to her senses. He thought that I was dealing with a huge unknown. He was very understanding to me.

Before Johanna knew, she was turning into their lane. Billy was outside, of course with his glove and ball. "Where is Daddy? Didn't you go to town to get Daddy? "

"No, Billy. I went to talk to the sheriff so he could help us look for Daddy. Now I need to talk to Mother and we both need to get ready for school. We will be late but I can still get there to take my test today. Where is Mother? Did you feed the animals?"

"Mom is in the house, trying to make breakfast. She sure is

slow today. And I did feed the animals, except Blackie, of course. I put Blackie's hay and water out, too, for when you came back."

Mother was in the kitchen, standing with an egg in each hand, staring out the window. The lard was sizzling in the pan and black smoke was beginning to rise.

"Mother, be careful. That lard is hot!"

Mother slowly raised her head to look at Johanna. "Oh, hi, Jo. I didn't see you come home. Did you find Sheriff Braun?"

"I sure did, Mother. He will investigate around town and down the shortcut if necessary. Now get to that lard before the house is ablaze. I need to run upstairs and dress for school. I will be a little late as it is. I think I can still take that math test."

"Please stay with me today, Johanna. I am so worried." She dropped the eggs in the pan and the oil splattered up.

"Ouch, the stove is way too hot." She pulled the pan off the burner quickly.

"Mother, I am worried about Father just like you. But I know that Sheriff Braun and Deputy Coffey will find him safe and sound. I need to take that math test today. Father would be so upset if I missed that test. I will take Billy to school also. He will be lost here in the house if he stays home. You and Mary need to wait at the house for Father to return. You need to be sure to play with Mary today. She is only four years old but she will sense something is wrong. She will miss Father as well. Play dollhouse with her. She loves to pretend that her dolls are all of us family. The corn husk doll is always Father when she plays. He is the biggest one, you know. That way, Father will be with Mary-- and you.

A faint frown formed at the corners of Johanna's mouth. A little tear welled up in her right eye. Her nose began to drip. She reached in her pocket and pulled out Sheriff Braun's hankie to wipe her nose. She hid her panic away from her mother's sight. "Sheriff Braun will find father," she said. "Sheriff Braun has to find him."

Chapter 11

Sheriff Braun filled in Deputy Coffey as soon as Pete came in the door. The two lawmen agreed that this behavior by Charles Stadler was highly unusual. Neither man could think of a single time in recent memory that Charles did not put his family first. He never stopped at the Wet the Whistle Pub after work, not even to celebrate a big event. Usually, a man would dream aloud about lands far away or going away to make a fortune. But for Charles his dream was always very simple: provide the best for Ellie and prepare the children for the best in life. More worry began to creep into the officers' heads. Charles must be hurt somewhere.

The plan was for Sheriff Braun to start out immediately looking for Charles. Pete would stay in the office for at least the first hour. Someone might call with news. Also, they knew that the first hour in the morning was when the majority of the calls came into the jail complaining about the mischief of the young ones or that night's missing drunkards. Pete would head out later if necessary and catch up with the sheriff.

First thing, John Braun walked straight over to the postal office. In her report, Johanna had assumed that Charles had been at his job yesterday. Sheriff Braun knew that one can't assume anything in an investigation. He needed to find some eye witnesses. He needed to retrace Charles' steps from yesterday. As he opened the front door of the post office the doorbell rang and Ralph called out from his desk in the back room.

"Is that you, Charles? Being early yesterday doesn't make up for being late today. There is a lot of mail here. You will be working your route until sunset tonight, young man."

Ralph scuttled out from the back room, a fistful of letters in his left hand. When he saw Sheriff Braun he added, "Oh, hi, sheriff. You looking for a particular piece of mail? I don't have everything sorted yet, John."

"Well, no, looking for some information, Ralph. About Charles. Sounds like you saw him at work yesterday? His family tells me he never came home last night."

"Oh, he was on his high horse yesterday morning. I came in at my usual time and he was almost done with all his sorting. He hooked up Old Grey and was off and running plenty early. And Old Grey was back in her place in the back stalls before I got back from my route. I didn't see Charles after that. And as you heard just now, this morning he has not shown his face here yet. Mighty peculiar, I say."

"I agree, Ralph. I am going to try to trace his steps of yesterday's route. Hope we find him real soon. You will have a long day today if you must deliver all the mail."

"I will get the mail sorted out first. Then, if Charles does not come by that time, I can call old George Collins who had Charles' route five years ago. He is slow since his heart attack, but the mail route will get done at least. I have a list of all the stops on Charles' west route for George to follow."

"Good luck, Ralph. Do you have a copy of that route I can use?"

"Sure. Here is a copy of the list. Kind of messy but it will do you fine. And good luck to you too, Sheriff."

Ralph had returned to the back room before the door closed behind the sheriff. Sheriff Braun paused on the front stoop of the post office, looking over the route list. The route headed out of town to the west and included all the farms on that side of the town. Ralph must service the east and town itself.

The sheriff stopped at the church on the edge of town first. This was the first stop on Charles' route. Sheriff Braun knew that Charles often stopped to talk with the young Pastor Jorstad before starting down the road and across the river. The Stadlers were not regular church goers but Reverend Jorstad had helped the Stadler family greatly after the death of Ellie's father.

The first thing John Braun saw as he entered the church was a big welcoming smile. "Hello, Sheriff. Are you resorting to prayer now to do your work?" Reverend Jorstad quipped.

"Might be a good idea, Pastor. Actually I am trying to trace the steps of Charles Stadler yesterday. He never made it home last night."

"Charles? I didn't see him yesterday. He must have been running early since he dropped off my stack of mail in the office while I was in the sanctuary doing my morning devotions and prayers. Most days, I am done and in the office when he stops by. I missed our little chat yesterday."

"Okay, Pastor. Please give the office a call if you see him. Have a good day. And put a good word in to the Lord for Charles today."

"Good luck, sheriff. I will pray for Charles today. You know you can talk to the Lord yourself while you investigate. Give it a try."

Sheriff Braun chuckled as he got into his vehicle. A quick little "Lord, please help us" flitted through his mind.

The sheriff meticulously retraced Charles route over the next hour and a half. Everyone had had mail delivered yesterday but few had seen Charles in person. Mrs. Nelson did confirm her conversation with him. She was so thankful for his encouragement during those last three weeks of illness, especially yesterday. He didn't seem to be upset or distracted at all. He was his same old friendly self, she reported.

Mrs. Hanson also agreed that Charles seemed himself yesterday. When he dropped off the bundle of mail at their house, he offered to help the men out in the back forty with the well-digging this weekend.

"Did he go back there to see Hans and Emil? "

"No, he told me he was rushed yesterday. He asked me to let Hans know that he would stop by Saturday to see if he could help with the well. I told him that the well should be done by then but thanks anyway. I mentioned to him that he was pretty early and he had smiled and said that he was looking forward to enjoying the beautiful afternoon playing with Billy and doing some fall garden tilling before sunset."

"Thanks, Mrs. Hanson. Greet your men for me."

The sheriff was done with his reconnaissance mission shortly thereafter and he headed back to the office. He made it back to the office in about two hours.

Pete had had one call that morning but it was not about Charles. It was a call from a very upset German farmer reporting that his dog had been killed on the road last night by one of those "speeding devil-machines." There had been no other calls.

Chapter 12

Sheriff had his plan worked out as he sat down to grab a quick cup of office coffee.

"Pete, we better head out to the river path and take a long look. Johanna mentioned that her father liked to take that shortcut into town and home again. He undoubtedly used the path yesterday to save time. I found no answers from the people on his route."

"No one saw him?"

"Oh, Pastor Jorstad missed speaking to him but had mail delivered. Mrs. Nelson said she had a nice conversation with Charles. Everybody got mail delivered yesterday. Mrs. Hanson recalled talking to him as well. All indications are that he was early and in a hurry."

Sheriff Braun changed his shoes to his hiking boots. That forest trail was studded with rocks and holes. He felt a nervous shiver as he laced up the boots. Those trusty boots had seen lots of heartache over the years. They were scuffed up and the sole of the right one was coming loose. He only put them on when there was a search. He had found plenty of bodies-- and other trouble --while wearing those boots.

The two men locked up the office and left a sign in the door window. They drove off in the sheriff's car and drove out to the edge of town where the trail started. Once the car was parked in the clearing next to the trail, they looked carefully around them for any clues. The fall leaves were everywhere and no footprints were visible.

"Over here," yelled Pete as he ran to a tree with a broken branch. Closer inspection revealed fresh signs where a deer had nibbled the soft buds. Oh, it was not a clue, just a sign of a hungry deer.

Each man stayed on his side of the path and concentrated on the path and the three feet next to the footpath. Nothing was out of place. No signs were seen of a recent human. On any other fine autumn day this would be a calming trek through nature. Not today.

After about a mile, they reached the point where the path crossed the river. Actually, the path stopped abruptly at the steep bank and the men were looking straight down a large log that had felled across the water. "This is Dead Man's Bridge," Sheriff Braun said. "I hate that name."

The river was rushing under the log, splashing against the many rocks studding the riverbed. In most years this river is more like a trickle in October. But this year three weeks of unexpected heavy rain had swollen the river into a vicious chute of roiling water.

There were signs of crossing on the log. Most people that attempted the crossing scooted slowly on their backside along the log while straddling it. The men thought they saw some evidence of this method now but of course they could not tell if the marks were there from Charles' trips to work and home or someone else's marks from the last few days.

The younger Pete hiked down the steep bank to the water's edge and searched for any human signs. He yelled back up. "No body, no clothes, no blood, no hat or torn fabric along here, John. I don't think his body would stay here for very long even if Charles had fallen. He would be way down the river by now if he had plunged into this mess. There is a deep pool here with nothing to snag a fallen object and then the treacherous current is racing downstream."

Sheriff leaned over carefully and peered down at the river. The rush of water brought on dizziness; he did not like heights at all. "You are right about that, Pete. Come back up. We need to get across this log though and follow the rest of the path. I don't like the idea of climbing out there on that log but we need to be thorough and, with the high water, this is the only way to cross the river here this year."

Twenty long, torturing minutes later they were on the other side of the water. The rest of the trip along the trail yielded no clues. Then, just ahead, they saw the opening of the trail on the county road and through the trees they could see the wisps of smoke from the Stadler chimney.

"Pete, you are the young one. Head on back to the car and

then drive around and out to the Stadler house the long way. Stop in at the office and check for any notes on the door. And call around to our neighboring towns and give them an alert, especially down river. I am going to go in along the trail and talk to Ellie. Be careful on that log bridge, too. I need you around here."

He smiled as Pete turned around. John saw a wet, messy patch on his deputy's rear with a cluster of leaves stuck on the seat of his pants. "I bet I have one of those patches, too," he thought, "I better be careful where I sit at Ellie's house."

Chapter 13

Sheriff Braun was not anxious to head to the Stadler home. He was now quite concerned about the disappearance of Charles Stadler. There had been no trace of him along the trail. No trace of anything.

Charles had been a bit of a free spirit in his early twenties, John remembered. The wanderlust bug had bitten him about ten years ago, sending him out as far as Colorado on one occasion. After Charles returned from that trip, John remembered many nights sitting at the bar at Smokey's tavern and listening to the endless tales of Ellie's beauty. During that solo trip the young husband had finally appreciated what he had in his wife Ellie and fell head over heels afresh. But the last few years he had not seen Charles near any tavern. Charles had dedicated his life to Ellie and the children. He had fallen into the rural mail carrier job rather fortuitously when George Collins suffered his heart attack and had kept that job ever since-- five years now. The steady income had probably saved that young man from disaster. The regular wage was less than it should have been but the Stadlers made ends meet and with their frugality they managed to provide a good home for the children.

John's mind wandered to the oldest child, Johanna. When she

came into the office that morning he thought at first that it was her mother Ellie. Johanna has really grown up since he saw her last. When was that? Oh, right, he just saw her last spring at the graduation ceremony for last year's seniors. At her age of sixteen, most teens developed life interests like college or an occupation and rapidly matured before your eyes. He wondered what expansive plans Johanna had in her heart.

As he approached the little house, Sheriff Braun saw Ellie and little Mary come out onto the front porch. For a moment they looked like little dolls in front of a miniature dollhouse. How can this family manage in such a small house? It must be so crowded. Ellie was dressed in her nightgown with a covering sweater; her hair had not been combed this morning. Mary was still in her pajamas.

"Did you find him, Sheriff? Is Charles alright?"

"Ellie, I am afraid we have not found Charles or any clues to his disappearance. May I come in and rest my bones? Find me an old, beat-up chair though so my muddy seat won't foul up your furniture."

Ellie cleared off a wooden chair by the table. She piled the breakfast dishes in the sink and sat down beside the sheriff, Mary climbing up on her lap.

"Ellie, we started at the post office. Ralph confirmed that Charles had gotten to work early yesterday and was off on his route well ahead of schedule. I checked all along the route and the regulars all confirmed that he had been through yesterday. Ralph reported that your husband must have gotten back to the office early in the afternoon and was gone before Ralph made it back from his route. Johanna had told us that Charles would have used the river hiking trail and so Deputy Coffee and I hiked the entire length right to the edge of the forest behind your house. Crossing that slippery log bridge was the trickiest part."

"Did you see anything at the bridge? I am so worried he fell into the river. You know he has had some dizzy times lately when he wouldn't eat properly and he worked extra hard. One day this summer I saw him almost staggering to the house, clutching anything he could to stay upright, and heading straight for the food cupboard. He had to sit there for almost half an hour before he felt like standing up again. If he was in such a hurry this morning he most likely skipped any lunch. I have scolded him repeatedly about not eating properly. Did you see anything there by the river?"

"That's interesting about Charles' spells there. I didn't know he suffered like that." He recalled the horrible dizzy feeling he had had as he slithered across the log bridge. "But, no, Ellie. We saw nothing there by the rushing river but sticks and branches in the angry water. The rains from the past weeks have swollen the river almost like it is at the spring thaw. The churning water was deafening. When we looked in the water we could not even see any of the big boulders down there. If he fell in there I am afraid we would see nothing of him."

"Did you call down to Riverton so they could check in the river there?"

"Deputy Pete is on his way back to the office and he will alert all the neighboring officers of the disappearance. But I must say that it now has been at least twenty hours since he would have crossed over the log bridge and I think any trace of his whereabouts would be long gone, even past Riverton. I am so sorry, Ellie."

"Sheriff, you must find him. Where did he go? What happened?"

"I don't know, Ellie. I don't know."

Ellie began to sob violently at that point. When Mary saw her mother's tears, she started to cry as well, hugging her mother and hiding her face from the sheriff.

After a couple minutes, Sheriff Braun reached over to put a soft, comforting touch to Ellie's arm. She looked up and wiped her face of the tears.

"Ellie, I need to ask some questions."

A long pause then she shifted her gaze straight into the sheriff's eyes.

"Ellie, did Charles ever talk about any ideas or plans to travel away?"

"No, we never discussed family trips because of our money

situation ------ Wait, do you think he ran away by himself?"

"Ma'am, I am just pursuing every possibility. I remember when Charles was younger, before he settled down and realized what a treasure he had here in you, he did quite a bit of traveling. Even got himself down to Denver one year, didn't he? Have there been any indications that he was thinking along those lines now?"

"No, Sheriff. None at all. He knew we couldn't travel. We needed all our money just to stay here. I need to stay home for the little ones and my extra sewing money has pretty well dried up these last few months".

"Ellie, I need to ask one more time. After a deep breath, "Would he go by himself, Ellie?"

"Oh, no. What are you saying? He loved us dearly. What are you implying?"

"I don't mean anything by it, Ellie. This is an official investigation and I just need to ask all the questions, even the tough ones. Maybe he has a scheme to make some extra money for the family. I don't think that's it, Ellie, but I need to do my job as sheriff and I need to ask."

"I am sorry, Sheriff, I understand. I am just so lost. Charles didn't come home last night. Charles..."

Another wave of tears hit both Ellie and Mary.

"Ellie, I see Deputy Coffey driving up now. We will head back to town and keep up the investigation. I will let you know anything I find out. And you let me know if you hear anything or think of anything."

Ellie couldn't even look up at that point. She just nodded and hugged Mary extra hard. A wave of nausea came over her. Her unborn baby was worried as well. "Oh, little one, I don't want to upset you,." she whispered. She reached behind Mary on her lap and massaged her belly gently.

Chapter 14

Johanna and Billy arrived at the schoolhouse an hour late. Jo explained the delay as best she could to both of the teachers. She apologized for their tardiness, knowing both teachers would have been worried sick about them. Her 20 years of teaching told Miss Anders what to do. She took Billy off to her room, immediately trying to get his mind off his father.

Johanna was so worried about her father-- but equally upsetting was the thought that she may have messed up her chances to take the big math test. Miss Block reassured her as best she could. The test had been scheduled to begin in a few minutes but Ms. Block decided then and there to delay the exam until the afternoon so that Johanna might be able to settle down emotionally. This was such a huge step in Johanna's plans for the future, she thought. Of all the students there at the school, Johanna was the only one taking this special math proficiency test. The more general tests would wait until afternoon also.

Billy just moped around the classroom the rest of the morning. Usually his bright face lit up when he saw his friends at school. Today he did not even look up when Joseph brought over the bullfrog he had brought to school. The frog had jumped right out of Joseph's hands and landed on Billy's shoulder but Billy just continued to look at his shoes. His eyes were dry but he looked so sad.

After lunch Billy had moments when he perked up. He raised his hand with the answers to several questions. He played tag with the other children on the playground. But as the hour approached for dismissal, his sadness enveloped him again. Miss Anders knew he was thinking about going home later to a house without his father. Billy loved his father so much. Charles was really Billy's best friend as well as his father.

Miss Block had been right about Johanna. The young girl was getting her resolve back after lunch. The teacher turned to her senior student and asked, "Johanna, are you ready to prove your mastery of the math material."

Johanna looked her teacher square in the eyes. "Miss Block, I have thought through today's trouble. Father is missing and that is so tragic. But I think he would be the first to say that to mess up this test would be even more tragic. I can hear him say just that. He has been so proud of my studies. He has been so good about helping me at home. Even though he cannot understand most of what I am doing with the math he loves to watch the process of solving the problem and the look on my face when I discover the right answer. I am ready to take on that test, for Father as much as for me. Can we start now?"

"Yes, we can. We have two and a half hours left of the day. I have arranged that you can use the back office where you will be able to concentrate as you should. The other students will stay at their desks to take their exams."

Johanna sharpened her two pencils again and followed Miss Block down the hall. She looked so determined.

'That girl is going to go places I have only dreamed of,' thought Miss Block. "Oh, the places she will go."

Chapter 15

The first afternoon

Ellie just sat in her chair, stroking Mary's hair. She could hardly summon up the energy to breathe at times. Why was this happening? Where is the good in this moment? Ellie had drifted away from the regularity of church attendance over the last years but all the childhood church language began to come into her head. Trust in the Lord. Faith. The goodness of God. "What goodness, God? Where is the goodness if Charles is lost? "she shouted. Then just as quickly as the questions came, Ellie's guilt jumped in. "I am sorry, Lord. I know I need to trust you."

It is a good thing that the hours of a day advance by themselves, for Ellie just sat and stared at the wall below the window-- stared at one nail in that wall. Finally, Mary stirred on her mother's lap, stretching her arms and legs after a comforting nap. "Mommy, I need to go to the bathroom."

"Okay, honey. Run along."

Ellie continued to stare at the nail. "Why, Lord, why?" She had still not heard a heavenly voice answering her one question. Nothing, she heard nothing.

The day crawled along like a fuzzy caterpillar crossing a path. Mary became the clock, her hunger announcing lunchtime and her crabbiness announcing nap time. All through the day,

Ellie listened for the big, booming voice of God giving the answers to her questions. She did not do a thing to clean up for the day--she didn't notice her nightgown or Mary's pajamas.

A sudden clomping of shoes on the porch startled her. Who is that, did Sheriff Braun find out something?

Billy burst in, out of breath, followed by his sister carrying both book bags. School was out.

"Is Father here? Is he sleeping?"

"Oh, Billy." Mother turned away. Her burst of sobbing told the children everything.

Eventually, Ellie could begin to speak again. "Johanna, how was the test?"

"Oh, fine, Mother. I did okay. It was hard to concentrate, hard to not think about Father."

For the first time that day, Johanna let her emotions come forth and the tears streamed out. Again Sheriff Braun's hankie came out.

Ellie realized at that point that she had not put together any supper. Her mothering instinct came forward and steered her to the pantry. Billy will be hungry soon. Her men were always hungry. She thought, 'Would she ever be able to say "her men" again.'

Chapter 16

Six days later

As those first days went by Billy showed no significant signs of coming out of his darkness. He moved like he was dream-walking, responding to no stimuli around him. He carried his glove around with him. The baseball was gone. He must have dropped the ball somewhere. He had no idea where. Each time he was out in the yard he would look down the road. When the weekend came he was no different. The odd-shaped stones and weird-looking branches that he usually collected and treasured lay on the ground in front of him unnoticed even when his shoe would kick them loose.

Ellie had gotten word out to Charles' parents using the Schultz' phone and six days later they arrived by train from Ohio. Mr. Whittingham from the train station brought them out to the farm in his auto. The usual Billy was not there with his excited greeting for Gramps. Gramps' secret handshake didn't even faze Billy that day; the boy just kept punching the center of his glove over and over.

Gramps and Ellie glanced at each other and Ellie shrugged and shook her head. She had hoped that Gramps could awaken the spark in Billy again. She turned away and laid her head on Grandma Stadler's shoulder. The sobs and Grandma's hugs began at the same time.

Gramps put his big arm around Billy and with his hand cupped on a shoulder he led his grandson off into the back yard. They sat down on the two big, round boulders peeking out of the ground near the woods. They had been named Mount Atlas and Mount Bigtop in the children's play.

"Billy, I am so glad to be here with you now. Grandma and I wanted to come first thing when we heard the news of your father but we had to find some neighbors to watch our livestock back home. The train ride seemed so much longer this time, seemed to take a month. I am so sorry about your father. I will miss him so deeply. He was my only son left on this earth."

"He is not gone, Gramps. He is just missing. He will come home soon. "

Gramps stared at Billy. The longing look in those young eyes was so familiar. His grandson at that moment looked so much like his son Charles had looked on that day over 30 years ago, the day Charles realized that his brother was gone forever.

"Billy, did you know that your father had an older brother?"

"No, Gramps, no one told me that. Where is he? Where does he live?"

Gramps hesitated briefly. Should I tell the story now? Is Billy ready for it? Am I ready for it? Or has there been enough sadness this week. Gramps decided to continue.

"O.K. Billy. I think it is time to tell you a sad story."

"I am so sad already".

"I know, young man. But this telling might help us both in the end."

Gramps began:

"Your father had an older brother named William. He was four years older than Charles. Your father worshiped his brother. He wanted to be with William every minute of the day. At school your father always wanted to be in the same class with William but of course the teachers had to keep them in different rooms because the lessons were different. Just like now with you and Johanna.

"We lived in Ohio then like we do now. Baseball was just getting its big start. The Cincinnati Red Stockings were to become the first professional team in the new National League. William followed that team in the newspaper so closely-sometimes his school studies suffered from it. He begged and begged to go to an exhibition game in Columbus and I finally said yes. I guess I was kind of curious about the game, too. The three of us, William, your father, and I took our buggy down to the game. The game was a great exhibition, exciting right to the end. By the time we left the field for home William had convinced me to buy him a big league glove, full regulation size. Your father also got a glove, one of the smaller junior-sized ones.

"Your father grew his love of baseball from William. William would toss the ball back and forth with Charles for hours sometimes."

"That's just like Father and me now, Gramps."

"That's right, Billy. Just the same."

"But one day a terrible accident happened. William was walking along the road home from school. He was alone that day as he had stayed to help the teacher split some wood for the pot-belly stove that kept the schoolroom warm. All at once, around the turn of the road, a carriage pulled by two horses came barreling out of control straight at William. The horses had been spooked by a flock of partridge along the edge of the road and the farmer could not control them at all. William had no time to move away and the horses trampled him badly. The farmer raced back once he had control of the team, scooped up William, put him in the carriage bed and rushed to town. The doctor could do nothing for the head injury that William had sustained. He died that night."

Gramps eyes welled up. He had not told that story for many years. The pain was still so sharp in his heart. Billy moved over from Mount Atlas to sit on Gramps' lap and seeing his grandfather's tears he cried and cried as well.

"Your father took a long time to believe the tragic story and even longer to come out of his sadness. He lost ten pounds from not eating during that stretch. But slowly he realized that shutting down in gloom was not going to help bring his brother back. One day he noticed William's official full-sized baseball glove lying in the corner of the barn. He tried it on his hand. It was far too big for his small hand but, to your father, it felt like it fit perfectly. He felt his brother William himself touching his hand inside.

"From then on, your father only used that big glove. That was the day that your father began to grow into a man. And, over the years, his hand grew into that baseball glove and he loved it. In fact the old glove that he uses with you now is that same glove from William. That is why it looks so old and is almost falling apart. But that glove is what kept your father from falling apart that summer, the summer your Uncle William disappeared."

A few more moments of hugs and tears went by, and then Billy raised his head and said, "Gramps, I'll be right back. You wait here."

The boy rushed into the house and in the mudroom next to father's work boots he found his father's ragged glove. Billy had always wondered why that glove looked so old and worn out. He ran back to Mount Atlas and jumped on top next to Gramps.

Gramps noticed the over-sized glove and recognized it right away. He reached over and gave Billy the biggest hug he could. He felt a forgotten burden lift from his heart. He brightened a little.

"Billy, now I know why your father wanted to give you the

name of your Uncle William. It somehow fits you just right."
Billy sat on his boulder in silence. Then his face came alive and his eyebrows rose questioningly.

"So my name is Billy but it is really William-- like my uncle?"
Gramps nodded.

By that time, Billy had picked up a ball-sized rock at his feet and tossed it to Gramps.

"Gramps, let's see if this glove will work for me." He fit his small hand into that old, broken-down 30-year-old mitt.

"I think it will be perfect. That glove was perfect for your uncle and it was perfect for your father and it will be perfect for you."

Billy inspected every angle and scuff of his father's glove. He felt how it held his hand so strongly, even if it flopped around loosely.

He caught the rock deep in the webbing.

"It is already perfect right now, Gramps."

Chapter 17

Since Charles was from the surrounds of Centerville and not the town itself, many townspeople did not know who the Stadlers were. The town-dwellers were mostly Easterners who had migrated there from New England or New York or Virginia. The farmers and rural-dwellers were dominated by the more recent immigrants. The Germans, Swedes, Norwegians, and Finns tilled the land and raised the crops. The children in the country went to the country schools. Most of the country families went to the ethnic rural churches. About the only interaction between these two groups was in the general stores and the shops. The farmers begrudgingly came into town to purchase the things they could not grow or create at home. The shopkeepers complained about the stingy foreigners. Why don't they buy the new goods we brought in for them? Since they came from Ohio, Charles' family would have fit more closely with the town people but Charles and Ellie had found a little house about 4 miles out that they could afford since Charles had found his job at the post office. They rarely attended church but when they did they went to the Methodist Church on the edge of town, Pastor Jorstad's church.

Sheriff Braun spent several days going through the town looking for clues to Charles' disappearance. He stopped in at each shop, each bar, even the library. Of all the townspeople, only Ralph the other rural postal carrier had noticed Charles the day he disappeared. Sheriff Braun knew that folks may have seen Charles on his buggy but paid no mind to it. The pastor at the Methodist Church, Pastor Jorstad, knew Charles had been by with the mail because it was on the table inside the door of the church but had not talked to Charles. Charles had not stopped in at any of the cafes in town. Sheriff Braun had shown the wedding picture of Charles to each waitress and each bartender as he went along. No clues. No one had seen him that day and no one had noticed him in the days before he vanished.

The Centerville newspaper editor kindly wrote an article in the weekly paper. It described Charles, mentioned his job as rural carrier for the environs to the west of the town, and explained that he had disappeared on Thursday afternoon October 15 without a trace. After a week, no leads had come into the office. Charles had vanished like a magician's assistant. Poof! Out of sight.

Sheriff Braun had to come to a formal conclusion in the case. He weighed the few facts carefully. Charles most likely did fall into the rushing waters of the river that afternoon. Braun and Deputy Pete Coffey had gone out to the river crossing several times looking over every inch of the trail and river bank. No traces. No clues. They called down to Riverton to report the incident and Sheriff Cooley had scoured the river down there. Sheriff Braun did not think there was anything more he could do. The river had claimed Charles as a victim. That was the official conclusion, the official statement.

There was Riley's Bog. This expanse of mucky, soft "quicksand-like" ground ran just off the trail that Charles had used. There were known cases of big animals that had wandered into the peat bog and sunk into oblivion. He had witnessed a sheepdog that had chased a rabbit to the edge of the bog. The rabbit had disappeared down a hole just before the muck but the rambunctious dog over-pursued and found itself standing in the middle of the soft ground. The more he struggled, the more he sank. A small companion dog had followed the chaser out onto the peat bog but was not heavy enough to sink down. Sheriff Braun had been on the other side and could do nothing but watch the frantic animal sinking in the bog. It took all his strength to hold back the owner from jumping into the muck to save the dog. One of the worst memories Sheriff carried with him was the muffled sounds coming to the surface as the big dog lost his struggle and the continual barks and whines of the little runt scampering frantically but safely on the surface. Braun had had nightmares for almost a year--nightmares where the dog-owner went down with his mutt.

If Sheriff Braun was honest with himself he truly thought that Charles had walked off into the sunset. He remembered

Charles' wandering streak when he was fresh in town sixteen years ago. The young man had harnessed that wild nature for many years now in his marriage to Ellie but human nature often seemed to have a habit of surfacing at the funniest times. Charles was alone a lot of each day while delivering the mail. Dreams and plans could have been worked through as the old mare trotted along the country roads. Maybe Charles was captured by his imagination on that beautiful day last week and bolted. A man wants to explore the world, doesn't he? Sheriff's own dreams of sailing the ocean came to mind. A man wants to explore his dreams.

Sheriff Braun's trips out to the Stadler farm grew sadder each time. There was nothing to tell Ellie and the children. Not one spark of hope was coming forward in the investigation. He told them the official report would mention the river and the peat bog. He did not broach the possibility that Charles had run away again. Those conjectures were better left unsaid. He would not do that to Ellie. He would not tie her up in knots.

Chapter 18

November 1, 1906

Ellie was a mess. She barely got out of bed each morning. Johanna was good about getting Billy to prepare for school. Jo found breakfast and made sure that her brother was dressed warmly enough. The walk to school each day was about three miles. Once in awhile a neighbor farmer would drive up behind and offer a ride in his wagon. Some days the children would jump in, some days they would walk along, politely declining the ride. But Jo had to make sure that Billy wore enough layers of clothes to keep the wind away. The family did not need any sickness right now.

Ellie, on the other hand, hardly moved in her bed. Little Mary was not an early-riser like most young children. She loved to lie awake at night and play with her rag-dolls in the dark and then sleep late in the morning. Usually about ten o'clock her empty stomach would wake her up and she would move over to her mother's room.

"Mommy, I'm hungry. Please get up now. The sun is shining and my stomach is growling."

Ellie would roll over in her bed, poking her face out at her little girl. A wave of nausea would announce to her that her littlest baby wanted attention, too. She would choke down her bile and would slowly sit up on the edge of the bed. Stroking Mary's silky hair soothed Ellie's stomach and she could pull herself out of the warm sanctuary of the blankets. She would head down the stairs and to the stove to make the morning oatmeal that Mary loved. A little piece of toast for Ellie, not so much for hunger as for settling the churning of her insides.

But after that little effort Ellie would just sit there in her chair and stare out at the front yard. She often would see an imaginary faded image of her husband walking up the lane. Never the real thing. Never the true essence of her partner. Never Charles' smiling face.

Sometimes Ellie would get Mary to dress in her day clothes. Just as often the two would live in their pajamas all day. Many mornings Mary would wander off to play by herself. Other times Mary climbed up on her mother's lap and snuggled.

During this time, the neighbors were wonderful. The word of Charles' disappearance spread quickly across the fields. A substitute mail carrier showed up each day. Unlike the indifferent townspeople, the rural community rallied around the Stadlers. Within two days the ladies came, presenting dishes of food for the Stadler family. They supported Ellie and the children as if it were a funeral. Many of the dishes that arrived Ellie had never tasted before. The German sausages with the spaetzel were familiar. But the Norwegian and Swedish fare was a new experience. Each wife had cooked the comfort foods that she herself and her family would want in a time of grieving. Sometimes the three children would balk at the supper in front of them but once they tried it they would discover why it was such a comfort food to the neighbor cook. A couple of the ladies must have organized everyone so that the pot luck arriving at the house was a proper mixture of main dishes and sweets. Ellie did not have to worry about providing food for her family. Actually she would not have worried anyway. All her waking time was a blur of grief for the loss of her husband, pressing down on her. More and more she thought about the permanent loss rather than the disappearance of Charles.

The neighbor men also pitched in and helped around the yard and barn. Several loads of hay and one of corn appeared next to the barn. The little garden of vegetables was harvested; the stacks of squashes and rutabagas far exceeded the usual cache as the neighborhood gifts were added to them.

The town, on the other hand, carried on as if nothing happened. Soon the townspeople forgot about the sheriff's questions. Soon the post office hired a replacement carrier and Ralph had help again. Ralph of course missed his old partner greatly but even he had never known Charles' family, had never been out to the farm. He did not think to go visiting Ellie and the family. What could he do there, after all?

Ellie had relied on Charles for news about the town. He had

come home each day spouting stories about the route and the gossip in town. Now no news came home.

Slowly Ellie began to notice less morning sickness. After a couple weeks she slowly began to eat better and recover some of the weight she had lost. She had more physical strength but her mind was still paralyzed. She did not notice that the air outside was getting more and more bitter. Winter was coming. The almanac predicted a true cold Minnesota winter.

Chapter 19

One month after

"Amazing, simply and truly amazing! "

These were the thoughts of Miss Block at the country school as she reviewed the teacher summary of the test results. Johanna Stadler had earned such a high grade Miss Block wondered if her star student had missed any questions at all. An extra page of praise had accompanied her test scores, written out personally by the administrator. Miss Block had never had a student receive such results on the conventional entrance tests and this test was so much more advanced.

"How could a young girl who was worried about her missing father do so well? Where did the strength come from? Johanna's father did not come home the night before and yet she was able to concentrate so well on the exam."

Miss Block had heard of people performing incredible feats of strength to save a loved one in grave danger. Johanna must have summoned the same fierce level of focus as she sat at the desk. Johanna had told her teacher about Mr. Stadler's constant interest in Jo's math lessons. Johanna had told her that each night during study time at home father and daughter would sit head to head as Jo worked through the solutions to her algebra. He was there even though he did not understand beyond simple calculations of multiplication and division. Miss Block pondered the test results one more time. She believed that Mr. Stadler was just as close to Johanna during that test in the schoolhouse as during homework.

When Johanna heard Miss Block announce that the test scores were delivered to the school she felt an immediate weight on her shoulders. "How terrible I must have done on that test--the very day Father disappeared."

Miss Block handed out the test results to each student. Johanna sat with the envelope in her hands, eyes closed and tears beginning to form. All her classmates ripped open their envelopes. Yells, shouts, grunts, sobs, even one loud swear word came from her fellow students. Johanna remained quiet.

Miss Block came over and put her hand gently on Johanna's shoulder. She did not want to betray the incredible results, but she needed Johanna to open the envelope.

"Please open your letter, Johanna."

Johanna slowly pulled the paper out of the envelope. Oh great! This must be someone else's results. Look at that near perfect score. She started to stand up to give the letter back to Miss Block. Then she saw her name at the top of the page. She stared at the perfect spelling of her name. Her name! Oh, my goodness! I did it! Father, I did it! We did it! Daddy, look at this score. I will be able to go to that school and study engineering. Oh, Father, where are you now when we should be celebrating?

Class was difficult to control for Miss Block that day, partly because of the excitement and disappointment of all the students. Mostly Miss Block was distracted by the amazing story of Johanna Stadler and her ghost father.

Ellie even perked up a little when she saw her daughter's huge smile and heard her acclamations way out on the front path. And when she saw the results she gave a great big motherly hug to Johanna. This was good news, the first good news for this family since Charles vanished.

Chapter 20

Six weeks after

Late November had arrived. Tonight the family was enjoying an animated discussion about school lessons. Billy had heard about Thanksgiving and wondered how the holiday came to be in November. Johanna reached for her civics book, turned to the chapter on national holidays and shared with the family.

In a decree during the Civil War, President Lincoln officially declared the fourth Thursday in November as Thanksgiving. Harvest celebrations had been around since colonial days as homage to the story of the Pilgrims and native Indians. Lincoln saw so much devastation and destruction of families because of the War Between the States. He perceived that a nationwide gathering around the dinner table after harvest time would serve to strengthen the families that were torn apart by the Civil War. In the proclamation he emphasized that all the American people "should support the widows, orphans, and families longing for the return of their loved ones from the battlefields." It was to be a day to heal; a day to bind together.

Six weeks had gone by since the day that Charles disappeared. Ellie was starting to wake up to the world. She was beginning to notice how out of touch she was around the house. She was determined to take care of the house and cook some of the children's favorite meals. Not every day. Not always very organized. She was amazed at how much Charles had helped around the kitchen; the dirty dishes used to fly away after supper, father and son with their backs to the table and their hands in the warm water. Now Billy and Johanna thankfully took that job to help Mother. Young Mary also jumped in, grabbing a towel to wipe the unbreakable dishes and put them up on the counter.

Ellie was getting grounded more and more personally as well. Her nausea was gone, her energy was returning. She had put a mark on the calendar on November 10 for the morning she had first felt the little one quicken. At first she just thought the feeling was her precarious stomach again but soon she remembered her previous pregnancies and the amazing moment when she had realized the kicking of life in her womb. This was it! There is no mistake about it. She had not told the children about the pregnancy yet. She better do that soon. Johanna was becoming a young woman quickly now. She was going to notice the changes in her mother one of these days.

The big question this mid-November was where was she going to get a turkey for the Thanksgiving celebration. In other years Charles was always successful at bagging a nice bird. She had heard that turkeys were very crafty in the woods but her husband was a special hunter. She would miss the roasted bird in the middle of the table, dressed and shiny golden and filled with stuffing. 'Hopefully the children will not be too disappointed without a big bird.'

A whinny and the rattling of a carriage came to her attention, waking her up from her daydream. "Who is that coming down the road? I don't recognize that buggy and team." She was accustomed to unexpected visitors; the neighbors were still bringing food donations every couple days. She felt so blessed to have such good neighbors. But this rig was a different color from any that had come before.

Edith Hanson smiled and waved as she dismounted from the buggy. The two horses were soon contentedly munching on the piles of grain she had dropped on the ground. She reached back behind her seat and lifted out a large package. As she climbed the three steps to the porch Ellie could see that the package looked heavy and unwieldy. Ellie rushed to the door and helped her neighbor into the front room. Edith's smile warmed Ellie's soul.

"Hello, Ellie. How are you? I am sorry it has taken three weeks for me to get back over here since I visited you with

Mabel Anderson. Fall is a busy time. Reverend Jorstad says hello as well. You remember him, right? He put this trip into my head. Here is a Thanksgiving goose for your family. We had extra this year and I don't plan to have a big meal next week. I know you may not feel like celebrating without your husband but sitting around the table with your three children will help with your healing. "

Ellie's eyes lit up when she saw the huge goose in Mrs. Hanson's arms. "Thank you so much, Edith. Charles always bagged our turkey from the woods. We were not planning a big deal this year either. His parents cannot come back over from Ohio now since they were here last month. Thank you from the bottom of my heart. But I have always heard that you folks sit before a giant feast at Thanksgiving. What is different this year?"

Edith turned away. Ellie could tell that her friend was beginning to cry, her sobs visible in her bouncing shoulders. She went over and reached around Edith's shoulders. A long hug ensued.

When she was able to compose herself enough, Edith turned back to face Ellie. "I will be alone this holiday."

"What in the world happened? What about Hans and Emil?"

A big sigh escaped. "Well, Emil left the farm last week. He and Hans were constantly fighting and yelling and cussing around the farm. He didn't say where he was headed but he took all his things. I suspect he finally decided to join his brother in Alaska. He was always talking about trying that adventure, too." She paused and looked away for a moment. After a big sigh, she said, "Hans will be the unwilling guest of Sheriff Braun until December. You probably heard that he has taken up the drink again. Taken it up real bad. And with the bottle always comes big trouble. Fights and more fights and now in the jail for two weeks."

"Oh, I am so sorry, Edith. I did not know. I do not hear any news. I always counted on Charles to keep me in the know. He was not a gossiper but he would tell me the important news each evening as we sat alone before bed. The children don't hear much out at the country school. So I had not heard anything. Oh, Edith".

Ellie sat them both down at the table, poured out some coffee and opened her heart to receive her friend's pain. Her own loneliness jumped to the back of her mind and her instincts as a helper took the reins. She realized that her friend needed her.

"At first Hans was just ornery again, coming home drunk every night. He would walk straight through the house to his bed, not even acknowledging that I was there waiting for him. Then one night I got a call from the Sheriff. Hans had gotten into a fight with a drifter during a poker game. The stranger had accused Hans of cheating and even of poaching some of his chips. The law had to break it up. Not one of Hans's old friends in the room defended him. Even his best buddy Iver had turned away in disgust. Sheriff told me that all the witnesses had backed up the stranger; Hans had indeed been stealing. Hans spent that first night at the jail. Sheriff let him out the next morning. When he came home my husband never said a word to me about it.

"Well, this kind of thing has kept happening and more and more frequently. Two nights ago Hans was caught inside the general store. He had crawled in the window and was rummaging through the drawers looking for the cash. Bought him two weeks in jail this time. Two weeks!"

Edith stopped speaking then, closed her eyes and folded her hands on the table. Her lips moved with her silent prayers. She paused slightly, looked up to the ceiling and quietly recited the Lord's Prayer. "Amen," she finally gasped, and her tears poured out.

"That is so sad, Edith." Ellie reached across the table and gently placed her trembling hands atop Edith's. The two women sat there like that for a long time---time enough for a calm to settle on the stack of weathered hands.

Edith needed to change the subject. "So----S'pose you heard about the new clothing store on Main Street. And the talk of a new opera house to replace the old Bijoux that burned down in June." Quickly Edith helped Ellie catch up on all of the news of the town. Edith and Hans lived on the other side of the river and much closer to town and so Edith got into town for shopping and church much more frequently than the Stadlers. Ellie had not left the house since Charles disappeared. By the time the clock showed three o'clock the two women were talked out.

Edith rose to leave. "Best be getting home."

"Edith, please join us for Thanksgiving dinner. We would love to have you here. "

Without a moment's hesitation Edith replied. "I would like that. I make a wicked pumpkin pie and apple strudel. I'll bring dessert."

Chapter 21

Thanksgiving Day

The Thanksgiving dinner table was looking splendid. Many of the neighbors had come by with their special holiday dishes. Ellie and Johanna had gone into the root cellar and found some amazing vegetables to fix. They picked the produce that would not make it through the winter and while they were down there they packed away the other pieces of their garden harvest so they would last as long into winter as possible.

Glazed carrots, green beans mixed with onions in a custard sauce, baked potatoes glowing a perfect color, all served on the best platters, surrounded the empty reserved center of the table. There was plenty of room for the goose. It was almost time to take the prized bird from the oven. Ellie's home-baked bread was steaming from the plate, cut into thick, inviting slices.

Billy reached out to accept the irresistible invitation wafting from the top piece of bread. Ellie smiled and gave a little guttural noise of "Uh, Uh. Not time yet, young man. "

"Mother, I am so hungry. All these smells are driving me crazy. Please let me have just one slice."

"No, we are waiting for Mrs. Hanson to arrive. You know very well we cannot begin without our guest." Out the window, they all could see Edith drive up with her carriage. She had a splendid, purple hat topped off with three long pheasant feathers. "Oh, look, there she is coming down the lane. Billy, come and help me pull the goose out of the oven. It is so heavy I will need your strong arms to hold the pan with me. "

They were pulling the roasting pan out just as Edith Hanson came up the steps. Johanna met her at the front door.

"What a gorgeous hat you have, Mrs. Hanson."

"Oh, it's nothing much. Just thought that such a wonderful dinner needed a bit of high class. "A ripping loud laugh followed by a snort caught even Edith a bit off-balance.

"Oh, gracious me. How vulgar that was!"

Ellie yelled over from the oven and rescued her friend. "Edith, that was just the sound we needed around here-- laughter."

"Johanna, can you help me with the desserts? Where is Mary? Oh there you are. I have a dish that is just your size, girl. Come with us."

A perfect parade of cheerful females ran down the steps to find the other goodies.

Two round dishes covered with cloths and suspiciously looking like pies and a square dish not hiding any of the delightful-looking apple strudel emerged from behind the carriage seat.

The golden goose, spilling dressing out of its back cavity, arrived at the center of the table simultaneously with the official unveiling of the pie and strudel.

Ellie greeted her friend, took her coat into the other room, and invited everyone to find their places at the table. "Edith, please take this seat at the opposite end of the table from me."

The three children stopped abruptly and stared at that chair. That was Father's chair. The whole family had avoided that seat since father disappeared. No one said a word.

Ellie broke the silence. "I know you are all missing your father today. I am terribly lonesome too. But Mrs. Hanson is missing her men as well this holiday and I invited her to be part of our family today. Everyone, please sit down."

"Mrs. Hanson did your son and husband disappear like Daddy?" Billy asked. (Ellie had not said a word to the children about Edith's family problems.)

"No, Billy, people can disappear in different ways. My son Emil has decided to travel the world and find his life path. Maybe he is up in Alaska with his brother. Who knows? My husband has been a very bad boy and he is gone too. He crawled into a bottle of booze a few weeks ago and hasn't come out. He is having his Thanksgiving with the sheriff and deputy---in jail."

"Wow, Mrs. Hanson, that is horrible news," blurted out Johanna. "I am so sorry about your troubles."

"It just shows us all that people can disappear in many different ways. I am so glad to be here with you today. Your family has been such a good example for the community. You have been so strong since Charles disappeared."

Ellie shook her head. "Oh, don't be silly, Edith. I have been dead like a scarecrow these weeks, sitting here in the house all day, barely able to take care of little Mary. "

"Oh, everyone has a shock when something like that happens. But you four have survived and are rising up to life again now with strength. I am proud of you."

Ellie walked around the table and hugged Edith with all her strength. Her eyes met each of the children's eyes and they rushed over all at the same time and hugged the two women. Billy brushed the bread plate off the table with his sleeve and started to cry in shame.

"Billy, don't worry, son, we have so much food today that we will not even miss the bread. So come and sit down, the food will be getting cold. Billy, as the oldest male here today and the "man of the house" you will be in charge of carving the goose. Be careful with that sharp knife."

Billy did the best goose-carving job any eight-year-old had ever done in that house. He nearly popped his buttons he was so proud.

As one can imagine, there was so much extra food that the leftovers filled every extra bowl Ellie could find. And no one missed the bread. Everyone was sitting there so satisfied. No one could move. No one could imagine even a bite of dessert going down right then.

A great weight had lifted off of each and every person at that table. A great calm filled the room. Later, Mrs. Hanson even fell asleep in the front room chair for a few minutes. Billy picked up his father's glove and put it on his hand. Ellie picked up the ball and tossed it in the air to her son

She looked up to the heavens. "Family will keep us going. Charles, we will be okay."

After Edith's nap the family gathered at the table again and shared the wonderful desserts.

The sweetness added to the calm atmosphere.

Ellie knew this was the moment she was waiting for. "Children, Edith, I have one more sweet thing to share today". Everyone groaned with the thought of more food. Ellie shushed them and with eyes sparkling she whispered "It's a sweet secret to share." She placed her hands down on her lower abdomen. "We are going to have a baby, our last beautiful child. "

Someone had once told Ellie that your love for a person can grow stronger in the absence of that person as much as in the daily presence. She loved Charles more today than ever before. He had helped create and nurture this incredible family. A weight lifted off of Ellie's shoulders. She stood taller and straighter.

Another gigantic hug was shared by all.

Later in the afternoon, while she was gathering the last of the dishes off the table, Johanna proudly watched her mother from across the room. She could recognize the little baby bump now that Mother had shared the news. "Thank you, Father," she mouthed to herself. "Thank you for this gift."

Chapter 22

December 7, 1906

The big thump of winter hit right after Thanksgiving. Twenty-two inches of snow swirled around the house, sculpting human-sized drifts.

The road was not visible from the front door of the house. Johanna and Billy shoveled all day to make a path to the barn and then over to the road. All that work was worth every ache they felt as the trip to feed the animals would be so much easier along the path than trudging through the deep snow. With this snow there was no chance that the children could get to school any time soon. Billy didn't mind that at all; ever since Father's disappearance he approached school as little more than a chance to play with his friends. Even that had soured a bit as the boys teased him about his father running away and not loving his family. Billy's violent denial that Father would run away on purpose just fueled the cruelty even more.

Johanna, on the other hand, was stressed out about missing so much of her last year of high school. She did not want to lose the edge she had gotten when she scored so well on the entrance exam. That incredible score motivated her to push forward even harder with her studies. She had been practicing her writing and speaking skills most recently, knowing that any good engineer needed to articulate her ideas clearly. She had a plan. During these stretches of days where the snow trapped them in the house, she would go up to her room and give speeches to her dresser and the dresses hanging in her closet. Ms. Block had also provided her with extra practice assignments including some hypothetical architectural engineering problems she had found in a trade magazine the last time she had been to Minneapolis.

Ellie increasingly felt better with her pregnancy. The nausea had completely lifted and her appetite was improving daily. The wonderful Thanksgiving dinner with Edith had started a friendship one could only dream about. Edith was so supportive and understood Ellie's predicament. Both women had lost their life mates. Both women craved the support they received from each other. Ellie was not sure she would have been able to survive this winter without that sisterly bond.

But now this snow was going to isolate her again. She had to be very careful she did not fall into her blues again. This was a good time to focus on Johanna and Billy a little more.

Back in town, every day Sheriff Braun found himself reviewing the events of that day that Charles Stadler disappeared. This whole affair was baffling. A family man like Charles had just vanished. It made a grown man ponder magic. Poof, Charles was gone. No trace. Sheriff had called downriver a few times to see if anyone had any new leads. He had contacted the large cities like St Cloud and Alexandria, even Minneapolis and St Paul. On a whim he even called the sheriff in Fargo to see if anyone new or unusual had shown up out there. He sent posters to all these places and more. He had walked the path through the woods many times, stopping particularly at the river log crossing and at the bog field to try to find any clues, as small as they might be, to Charles disappearance. He had found a beat-up old hat at the edge of the peat bog one day but Ellie had said that Charles never owned a hat like that. As hard as it was to comprehend, Charles Stadler had left no traces.

Nothing unusual had sprung up around the town. There had been a string of minor burglaries at the end of October. It turned out that Hans Hanson had started on the bottle again and was looking for little things he could sell to buy his liquor. That man had been a troubled man before he had met his wife Edith but she had found a way to tame him and his urges. When the oldest son Hans, Jr. had jumped off to Alaska Hans had binged for a couple weeks but then had just disowned the young man. Luckily, Hans had managed to stop the drinking then. But this time the Devil whiskey had grabbed him tight. Booze is such a tough opponent in a person's life. Now Hans had earned several stints in the jail cell; he was hardly home anymore.

Reverend Jorstad had mentioned to Sheriff Braun that Ellie Stadler and Edith Hanson had developed a nice supportive friendship. That was good for both of them. Sheriff Braun was not much of a churchgoer himself but the peace that some Christians gained from the church was hard to ignore. Sheriff Braun thought about little Billy. I need to check on the boy, maybe take him out fishing or hiking. He needs a male in his life. I know, I'll take him to a baseball game. He loves baseball. As soon as I can get out to that house I will go visit. The waist-high drifts along Main Street made him chuckle. Not right now though, the snow was way too high on the rural roads, especially north of the river where the Stadler home sat. I'll need to wait until the sleigh traffic packs down the snow and creates a harder surface. And the baseball game will come this summer. It is too bad that Charles' parents live so far away over in Ohio. They cannot possibly come back over here to Minnesota any time soon.

Chapter 23

Two months after

Edith and Ellie really started to bond after the Thanksgiving dinner. Edith had a sleigh that could navigate the snow-covered roads pretty well and Billy and Johanna trekked out to meet her along the road a couple times so she had company as she approached the house. Billy loved holding the reins and giddy-upping the horses.

Edith asked the family to church in mid-December and the four Stadlers dressed up in their Sunday best and rode into town to Pastor Jorstad's church. Ellie vaguely remembered attending church with her father back in Ohio. The children had never gone to church. The church words were like a foreign language to them all. But the feeling of calm and security that they felt from Edith seemed to bubble out of each of the other parishioners in the church. Pastor Jorstad was nice too. He spoke so plainly and eloquently about this season of waiting for the Baby Jesus to come. He stopped to speak to them after the service.

"Hello, I am Pastor Jorstad. Edith has told me about your trials this year. I am very sorry. But I am so glad to see you here now. I hope you felt comfortable and not too lost in the liturgy. I did notice that you, young lady, were singing along with the hymns." Johanna beamed shyly.

"I sang along with *Silent Night*," piped up Billy. He had learned that hymn in school just the previous Friday.

"That was the nice male voice I could hear. These Minnesota men don't open their mouths much. They don't think it is a man's place to sing a gentle church hymn. They will belt out on *Joy to the World* on Christmas Day, though. It is nice to blend in other new voices. Say, what do you have there?"

"That's my baseball glove. It was my father's glove until he disappeared. And before that it belonged to my Uncle William. I was named Billy in honor of my Uncle William."

"That is a nice memory, Billy. I bet you are anxious for spring and green grass so you can play ball again."

"But Father is gone. Who will I play with, Pastor?"

"We will find a game for you. We have many boys around here that like to play. "

Excitement built on Billy's face. His eyes sparkled, his eyebrows raised. Then, Pastor Jorstad saw the darkness spread across the boy's face.

"Don't worry, Billy. No matter where your father is now, Billy, he will know you are doing your best. He will be very proud of you, very proud of his young man."

"Time to get going, Billy. Thank you, Pastor, for talking to my boy. And thank you for the wonderful welcome we feel here at your church."

"You are always welcome here. And Edith will tell you that this is not my church but it is God's place. He provides the peace in these walls. Don't forget to bring that pretty little girl hiding behind your skirt. What is your name, young girl?"

Surprisingly, Mary jumped right out from behind her mother and sang out, "My name is Mary. And it is much easier to remember than Billy-Uncle William over there."

"You are right, Mary. That is a very special name, too. That is the name of Baby Jesus' mother in the Bible."

"Wow! I am special, mother. Did you know that when you gave me that name?"

"Oh, right from the first time your father and I saw you we knew you were the most special little girl we could hope for."

Mary beamed a smile that only a four-year-old girl can produce, twirled around twice to make her dress spin outward and jumped forward even more.

Pulling out her big husk doll that she had carried to church she proclaimed, "And this is Daddy Doll. And he is keeping us all safe while Father is gone."

With that, everyone was speechless, frozen by Mary's innocence.

Pastor now turned to Edith and thanked her for bringing the new family to church.

The four visitors climbed up into Edith's sleigh with her. Off they went. For just a little while that morning they felt so calm and blessed.

Sitting on the back bench of the buggy, Ellie treasured her trip to church that Sunday. I wish Charles could have been here today. I think he would have felt good in this sanctuary. This place is not like the stuffy, Lutheran churches he attended as a young man.

Billy leaned over to his mother and whispered," See, I told you I should bring my glove today. That is my little piece of Daddy. Daddy was there today in the glove, too, just like in Mary's doll. I just know it, Mother."

"Yes, Billy, I think you are right."

She had to turn away to hide her tears but they were a different kind of tears. They were tears of sorrow mixed with tears of calm, friendship and peace. And her pride in her children.

Edith couldn't stop smiling after she dropped her friends off at their house. The hugs and kisses warmed her troubled heart. She missed her boys and her husband terribly much but she felt like she had been with family that day. "Thank you, Lord."

Chapter 24

Christmas Day, 1906

Snow and wind continued to pummel this small Midwest community. Drifts rose to cover the wind break bushes along the roadsides. Only the sleighs and horses could make their way through the roads; no motor cars this time of year.

Edith did not see her husband Hans at all that winter as he had been arrested so many times that he had been moved to the larger prison in St. Cloud. She felt terrible and alone without her family, especially during this holiday time. Edith invited the Stadlers to Christmas Day services at the church but there was no way that they could make their way into town that week. Nonetheless, she was determined to go see the Stadlers at all cost. It was a slow and dangerous trip over to the small house the day of Christmas. The horses wanted no part in this folly but she cajoled and demanded, bribed and coaxed and somehow they all got through the drifts on the roads. Her sleigh was loaded with lots of presents: old toys and clothes that her boys had played with many years ago and jars of produce she had canned last summer. (She had noticed that the Stadler dinner table was getting bare of vegetables and fruit desserts.) She pulled up to the little house finally in the mid-afternoon.

What a surprise for Ellie to see that wonderful smiling face come to the front door. "How did you get over here, did you fly over the snowdrifts? " Ellie grabbed her friend's coat and hat and hurried her over to the fireplace to thaw out her cold fingers.

"Oh, my old horse team doesn't really know any better. They almost seem to enjoy the extra work of pulling through the drifts." Secretly she was relieved that she made it through and embarrassed that she had tried it at all. "Johanna and Billy and Mary, will you please bundle up and bring in the packages out in the sleigh? Don't peek! "

The three children rushed over and put on their coats and boots. "What could all this be, Johanna?" the young ones whispered.

"We will just have to wait and see," big sister chirped. "Now you heard what Mrs. Hanson said, no peeking!"

"We so wanted to come to your church for the Christmas worship, Edith. I imagine that the place was so pretty with candles and Christmas trees and boughs. I am sad that you were not able to be there either."

"Oh, Ellie, we will make a beautiful church service right here. We will make church right here where our big family is. If your older children can find a small tree out in back I might just be able to decorate it all the way to the top with tinsel and candles. And we will find materials so that Mary can help us make an angel for the top. We will have a good Christmas; as good as we can with our men missing. We will sing so loud on the Christmas songs that Charles and Hans will be able to hear wherever they are."

Ellie began to tear up but the door flew open and the noisy children jumped in with arms filled with bundles.

Billy was overflowing with enthusiasm. "I didn't look, Mother. I didn't peek even once. One of the bags split open and a bunch of jars of pickles rolled out on the walk.
But, Mommy, I did not take a single peek, I promise."

Mary even spoke up, "I did not look in this bag with the fancy paper wrappings. I didn't look at the four presents in there."

Ellie and Edith beamed like mothers and shared the hugs of the children. Before the older two children unbuttoned their coats Mother asked them to go out with the saw and find a small fir tree in the yard, one about the height of Billy.

Dinner was simple but nice. Warm soup and fresh bread and apples and milk. And a newly-opened jar of homemade pickles that had rolled out of Billy's sack.

After dinner Billy checked to see if the tree was dry. Perfect. The scrawny tree was decorated as Edith had promised with sparkling tinsel and small tree candles and some little decorated boxes that looked like presents. Then Edith found some white paper and helped Mary roll up a cone for the angel body to fit over the top spear of the tree. Mary ran upstairs and found an old doll in her room that was ripped at the waist and Edith cut it down and attached the waist to the paper cone. Johanna drew a pretty smiling face on the faded doll and Ellie and Billy attached a piece of gold trim on the top of the blonde head to serve as the halo.

"Look Mother an angel on top of the tree," Mary exclaimed proudly.

"Yes, our guardian angel."

The exchange of gifts topped off the day. Billy discovered hats and shirts and shoes from Edith's long-grown boys. Johanna opened to find some new books to read and an empty diary book that Emil Hanson had never used. Mary discovered four dolls that Edith had made for faraway nieces when they came to visit but had never been used. And Ellie could not be happier with the huge harvest of food that would replenish her emptying pantry. Edith opened a prayer shawl that Ellie and Johanna had crocheted for her. And Billy had constructed a wooden keepsake box and he and Mary had filled it with little strips of paper naming tasks that they promised to do for Edith around her house and yard next year. Just last week the young ones had painted a cross on the top of the box--a cross like the one they had seen in church.

Edith had brought her Bible along and she opened it to the story of the first Christmas. "Johanna, will you read the story for us?" Edith implored.

In her beautiful, well- practiced presentation voice Johanna gave a beautiful reading. Music followed with *Silent Night* and *God Rest Ye Merry Gentlemen* and *Joy to the World*. Ellie began the first carol at such a ridiculously high pitch that they all began to giggle and stopped singing. Johanna put her hands up to get control of the choir and began *Silent Night* several steps lower. Everyone agreed that Jo was the correct director for the ensemble and she started the other songs as well. Edith bowed her head and each Stadler did the same and, with Mary up in mother's lap and the fire warming everyone, Edith prayed to God about the loss of Charles and Hans, prayed that by some miracle, they would each find a way to come home this year.

Before the prayer was finished, Johanna jumped up from her chair and stormed up to her bedroom. Her crying and yelling poured out of her room. Ellie began to rise, but Edith caught her eye and motioned palms out---let the young girl alone, mother. Ellie nodded a tiny acknowledgment. Ellie knew that Johanna had not let all her pent-up worry and emotion about her father escape. Billy and Mary squirmed in their seats a little and peeked through their half-closed praying eyes but they didn't dare move.

Edith continued praying, "And keep all of my friends safe through this coming year. Please help Johanna and Billy and little Mary and Ellie to move on in their lives without Charles. And we can't forget that little unseen baby in Ellie's womb.

Keep Ellie and that baby safe at the time of delivery."

"Thank you, Father, for the gift of these friends and their love for me. In Baby Jesus' name, Amen."

Chapter 25

The calm that Ellie felt on Christmas filled her and steered her through the next several days. This was the first of January, the coldest of the cold time, in Minnesota. The wind howled in the trees, stirring the snow off one drift and unto another. The movement of the tree branches was the only life one could see out the windows. The birds were hiding elsewhere. But Ellie was at peace.

Two days ago, a bright sunny day, she saw a big patch of green out in the front yard. A cool summer breeze blew through the green leaves. Was that a song bird she heard? Then she awoke; sitting in the rocking chair, with Mary snuggled on her lap. A dream. A dream like nothing she has had since Charles' disappearance.

Ellie reflected on the Christmas her family had had with her new friend Edith Hanson. That woman was such a blessing to us, such a help at this time. The children were so happy to see all those wonderful presents she brought. She noticed that the time that they were preparing their gifts to her was even more joyful. As each of the little ones wrote out a promise of service for Edith, the other would marvel and think of another chore even better. These were chores, didn't they know. They were never this cheerful about chores. And Johanna loved the chance to learn how to knit the prayer shawl. She looked like a little grandmother, sitting in the rocking chair with the half-completed shawl spread on her lap.

There was something else, though, that Edith gave us. Despite the terrible circumstances in her family, the troubles Hans was experiencing and the loss of her last son, she remained so grounded. She was so giving of her time and resources, but most importantly, her love. Ellie knew that this love came from Edith's deep faith in the church. Her prayers on Christmas Day were spoken as to one's own Father, not to a distant, unseen God.

Ellie went up to her bedroom, checking on Mary napping snugly under the down blanket. Ellie gently moved the little girl's right foot back under the warmth. Such an angel.

In her bedroom, she rummaged through the bookshelf in the corner and, under a stack of picture books, was her Bible. Ellie pulled out the large leather-bound book and carried it down to the front room. Stoking up the fire first, she settled in to re-acquaint herself with this volume that she hadn't opened for years. She drew it up to her nose and took in the musty air. She hoped that the words inside were not as stale to her.

Ellie had never been much of a churchgoer. Her mother was the religious one in her family. Once in a while she was able to get Father to go to church but usually he would disappear out to the barn or out to the fields just before the time to wash up for services. When Ellie's mother died, Ellie was only seven. Her aunt and uncle took her to their church for a while but, as often happens, that habit fell away. Ellie always kept the Bible in her room but was too interested in her story books and school lessons to open the volume. However, she did remember vividly how much enjoyment that the Bible readings gave to her mother. The look on mother's face would soften and a certain sparkle came to her eyes. In fact, Ellie just realized, this is the same look I saw in Edith's face on Christmas as we heard Jo read the passages about Baby Jesus. The very same peacefulness.

Ellie held the big book in both hands and let the pages open on their own. With the book lying in her two palms, she looked at which place the book had chosen. Moving a photo aside, she was amazed to see that she was reading the Christmas story in Luke's gospel. That must have been Mother's favorite place. She sure liked to read it to me. Before delving into the words, she looked more closely at the picture. There was a formal sitting of her family, Mother, Father, and her as a little baby. On the back was the word "precious." A tear formed in her eye. She found her handkerchief in her apron.

The passage in Luke was still familiar from the reading on Christmas. Ellie was struck by the enormity of that scene, singing angels and worshiping shepherds all for this little baby. And the family was so poor. We are not the only ones.

Ellie noticed a piece of yellowed paper stuck a little further back in the Bible. Carefully, she folded the book open to that place and took out the paper. It was brittle like a dried maple leaf in late fall. A small tear appeared as she unfolded the paper. It was a letter written to her mother from Ellie's grandfather. The date on the top was just one month before Ellie was born. Wow! As she read the script she realized that this letter was telling Ellie's mother of the sudden sickness and death of her own mother. The phrase "we have lost your mother" burned a hole right through Ellie's heart. Oh, my goodness, how did Mother manage? She must have been devastated. Mother lost her beloved just like I lost Charles. How did she survive?

After a long cry, Ellie looked down again at the book. There was a sentence that was under-lined here at the end of Matthew. "And lo, I am with you alway, even unto the end of the world." As she examined her grandfather's letter more carefully, she saw written on the bottom of the last sheet a list of Bible verses. The first one was this very Matthew passage she was turned to. Second on the list was in Matthew again, in the fifth chapter: "Blessed are they that mourn, for they shall be comforted." The last one was Romans 8: 38-39. Ellie found those verses further back and read the underlined passage "nothing can separate you from the love of God in Christ Jesus." These are the messages that kept my dear mother going. These must be the words that Edith clings to as well. Maybe they can help me, too.

As Ellie replaced the Bible back on the shelf she noticed several other books next to the space for the Bible. She pulled out the thinner books gently, seeing that they were old like the Bible. She had a stack of five on her lap. As she paged through these stories she began to have memories of the wonderful stories that her mother read to her each night in those years before her death. Here was "Tales of Mother Goose" and "Rip Van Winkle." One of her favorites at age six was "The Swiss Family Robinson," about a family that was shipwrecked on an island. And here was "Little Women". I must start to read this to Mary. Meg and Jo, I loved them. Who were the other sisters? Paging through the pages she discovered Beth and Amy. When Ellie saw the name Jo the last time she wondered out loud, "Is this why I named my first-born child Johanna?" The bottom book looked almost new. "Hans Brinker and the Silver Skates" was written in 1865. That was just a few years before Ellie was born. Maybe Mother was saving this one for me later. Looks like a story of a Dutch boy and skating. Looks fun for Billy.

Something broke her spell and she turned to find Mary at her bedroom door, still sleepy from her long nap. Ellie motioned her girl over and showed her the books, telling her they were from her own childhood. Mary wanted to read them right away but Ellie told her that it was time to start making the supper soup. "We will read them soon. Oh, I am so excited to share the characters with you, little one."

With that, she placed the books in the kitchen on the top shelf of the pantry. At supper that night, she announced that she had a secret to share. Mary began to speak, but Ellie signaled for her to be still so it would be a surprise. Each of the books was presented with a short description. "Now, these treasures will be on our bookshelf in the front room but we all have to be extra careful because these books were made long ago when I was a child."

Billy piped up, "Boy, they can't be that old."

Posing as a crippled old crone, Ellie made everyone laugh like they hadn't in ages. Even the baby, cramped in her womb, kicked in delight.

Chapter 26

Three months after

Storms of confusion and anger began to surface in Billy's life after Christmas. His generally helpful personality started rebelling whenever Ellie asked him to help around the house. "I don't wanna," he would whine. "I don't have to do that." He kept the baseball glove near him as much as possible; he banged his fist harder into the pocket each day. The previous night Billy's face showed pain after the last fist smash.

"Why did Father leave us? Where did he go? When is he coming back? I want my father right now. "

"Billy, I ask those same questions from the time I rise to when I lay my head down again on the pillow. Every day. I haven't found an answer to any of those questions yet. "

"Do you think those prayers that Mrs. Hanson said at Christmas will come true? Will they bring Father home?"

"I wish I knew. No matter how hard it is, we need to wait and see. I wonder if it would help that each time we were mixed up or mad or confused that we said the same silent prayer right then."

"But I don't want to bow my head or get on my knees in front of everyone. That would be silly-looking. The boys at school would tease me, Mother."

"Oh, you can just pray the words in your head like whispers and keep doing what you are doing. The boys will not guess what you are doing. Reverend Jorstad told me he does that all the time, in the grocery store or during his church meetings. Will you promise me that you will try? And after the little prayer you could ask God if he can help you be more helpful to your teacher and here at home. You know that you are my big man now and you need to do some of the things that your father did around here. Just 'til he gets back, I mean. Bringing in the firewood is so helpful and each time I see a load of wood that you carried to the fireplace I can almost see Father in front of me. "

"I will try, Mother. "

Ellie wasn't finished. "Is everything going O.K. at school, Billy?"

"Oh, sure, Mother." Billy did not make eye contact.

Billy's face and posture told Ellie that she should really get over to see his teacher. Hopefully the roads will clear enough so I can drive over there soon, Ellie thought. I suspect Billy is having some trouble at school.

She jostled his hair lovingly and said, "Well, please run out and get one of those big loads of wood for this afternoon. Try a little one of those prayers while you walk; don't fall, pay attention to your feet."

Billy laughed at the picture of himself falling in the snow bank.

"All right, Mother. I will do my best."

Ellie discussed her concerns with Edith later that week. Edith reported that the roads were improving since there had been no recent storms. She suggested that her larger carriage could make the trip to the school, and after that, as long as they were venturing out, even all the way into town.

Tuesday the weather was clear and the sun was out. The women bundled up and piled into the carriage, heading to the country school where Johanna and Billy attended. That morning Jo had taken a note from Ellie to Billy's teacher asking for some private time to talk about her son. Miss Anders had arranged with Miss Block to be ready and free when Ellie came. Miss Anders greeted Ellie warmly, taking her coat and hat and scarf. She turned to Edith and suggested she could visit the back of the schoolroom with little Mary. They quietly sat down on the reading rug with a storybook.

Ellie got right to the point. "I came to see if all is well with Billy here at school. How is he interacting with his classmates? I have noticed a change in him lately at home."

"You are a very observant mother, Mrs. Stadler. Yes, Billy has had a bit of trouble with a couple boys. They have been teasing him about his father running away, even saying that his father did not want to live with your family anymore, that maybe he had a girlfriend in another town. Several of them, including his best friend Henry Carlson, have been calling Billy Little Orphan Annie on the playground. Boys can be brutal, especially when they see they have power over someone."

"But that is all falsehoods. All we know about Charles is that he did not come home that night in October. We still hope we will see him again."

"Children this age usually parrot what they hear at home, Mrs. Stadler. The rumors are inevitable. The gossips will get tired of the topic as soon as there is a new juicy rumor to spread."

"Well, thanks for the information, Miss Block. I will be able to speak to Billy now about these things. At home I am working to help him take over some of the "man" chores his father did each day. Maybe a discussion in class about adjustments and changes surrounding such a loss would help. Do you know that Henry's uncle died in a farm accident? If all the children were included in those lessons the bullies might not be so brutal."

"Absolutely. We have been planning just such a lesson for later this week. By the way, when is the little baby due to arrive? That is a nice little bump in your belly."

"Oh, I calculated late-April for the due date. Being the winter and all, I haven't even been in to see the doctor or midwife yet. Guess I know what to expect since this is my fourth time around."

"Well, please let me know if I can help in any other ways. By the way, that daughter of yours Johanna is a real gem. She is such a good student here. And her dream of being an engineer is amazing. That dream keeps driving her to excel. And she is like a second teacher in our upper classroom. "

"Johanna is very special to me...ahh...us. Thank you for taking the time to talk with me today. I best move on now. Edith Hanson is going to take me into town this afternoon to shop for supplies. Can you believe I have been to town only once since Charles disappeared and that was on a Sunday morning?"

Billy watched his mother come through the room. He knew that she had talked in the back room with Miss Anders. They must have discussed the fight with Henry. How did Mother find out about that? He figured he was in big trouble. As Ellie walked past he blurted out, "I didn't do anything wrong; I just bopped Henry in the nose when he called me a name, a really bad name.

Ellie stopped and gave her son a little squeeze of the shoulder and a big smile. "I know, Billy, I know."

As she shook hands with the two teachers she whispered to herself.

"My big man. I need to protect you, Billy."

Chapter 27

Maybe it was the fact that Billy saw his mother speaking to his teacher. Maybe it was the conversation that Ellie had had with him about his new "man" responsibilities. Maybe he was saying little silent prayers as he worked around the homestead. Something turned a switch on in Billy. Something made a difference. He became very diligent about the firewood. He fed the horse each day and watched over the other animals in the barn. He practiced his nightly reading and his spelling and ciphers. He cleared the dishes after supper with Johanna and seemed to enjoy the talk with her as they washed them up in the kitchen sink. He was Ellie's "little man" now... His teacher sent home a note recounting how his work at school had improved greatly since Ellie's visit. He had in fact started helping his tormentors, even Henry, with their math and reading. He had his friends back again.

Johanna continued to excel at school as well. She was now correcting papers for the lower grades at night, bending over the stack of work, writing comments in red pencil in the margins. She progressed in her own math and geometry studies, too. For Billy's sake she would often ask him to help her with the math calculations. This, of course, slowed her down in her work but she knew it was boosting Billy's confidence. Billy was learning his ciphers quickly.

One night Ellie looked over at the table and saw two heads bent over a work paper, hair almost touching and she saw a vision of Charles and Jo deep in thought. The glow of the fire was flickering in their hair. A murmur could be heard from the table. A bittersweet smile appeared on her face. 'I miss Charles so much, but these children are such a strong reflection of his presence. I am so thankful for them right now.'

Little by little, Ellie worked on the preparations for her new baby. She had Billy drag the cradle in from the hayloft. He wiped it clean and polished all the wood to a new shine. Johanna went up in the attic and found the petite bedding for the bed. Double washing brought them back to baby softness. Mary drew several pictures for the new baby, pictures of the family and the small farm site and a very special picture of the Christmas tree she remembered from this year. Mary had saved the homemade tree angel and Ellie was able to attach it to the head of the cradle "to watch over the baby and keep it safe."

"Can we name the baby Charles, after Father's name?" asked Billy.

"You are so smart, Billy. Yes, that is my plan, young man. If the baby is a boy, that is. What could we do if the baby is a girl?" She giggled teasingly.

Billy scrunched up his nose in thought. He had not imagined that another girl would invade his world. Ellie could see the calculations spreading across his face as he pictured his world with three sisters. "We have a girl in the grade below me in school whose name is Charlotte. That has part of Father's name in it. That would be good. If it's not a boy."

"Billy, that would be great," Johanna and Ellie chirped at the same time. Ellie finished, "Wonderful idea! Charles or Charlotte. We have the name all set."

"Maybe you have twins, Mother," laughed Billy mischievously.

"Oh, you be quiet, you little troublemaker. That joke is not funny. Twins."

She turned back to the stove to finish supper. Her hands naturally found their way to her baby bump, rubbing her dress quietly. "Twins, we don't even have room for one more in this little house. What could we do with twins?" she mumbled softly.

Chapter 28

End of January

By the end of January, Edith was able to take Ellie into her first doctor's appointment. Doctor Holman confirmed the due date to be the end of April. He thought everything was progressing well. Ellie's weight matched up with the growth chart in the doctor's book even though she had eaten so little during her early weeks of depression.

The baby was moving vigorously that day; in fact, it felt like a herd of cattle in there, kicking up a stampede. The nurse and midwife reviewed the pregnancy and the recommended diet. Most likely, one of the midwives would get out to the house for the delivery rather than Ellie driving into town while in labor. Hopefully the weather and the roads would cooperate. It felt good to be talking with these new voices. She listened attentively and took some notes to review later. When she returned home she vowed she would begin walking around and around her home each day while Mary was resting in the afternoon so she would build up her strength for labor. In the back of her mind, Ellie inventoried the neighbor women who could be summoned in an emergency, the women who had experience with home deliveries.

Throughout the remainder of winter the two women made

sporadic trips to town to see Dr Holman. Each time they also stopped at the general store for household supplies and food. Ellie was getting more concerned each trip that the supply of cash that she and Charles had stashed away would soon run out. The simple life they lived had allowed the couple to save what they thought was a nice nest egg for a trip with Johanna to take her to start college next year. Now those funds were almost gone. Without Charles' weekly income the family had nothing coming in to pay expenses. If the wonderful neighbors, and especially Edith, had not been so helpful this winter the money would have been gone long ago.

Edith found a neighbor family that needed some help around the house and introduced them to Johanna. Johanna went over each weekend and earned a little cash. She helped cook for the large crew of dairymen that milked the cows each day. The wife would do much of the baking and weekly food preparation on Saturday and store the food out in the entry of their large house that served as her pantry.

Johanna was a good worker, appreciated by all. She put all her earnings into her mother's coin pot. What will my family do when I leave for my new school? I so want to go to college next fall. But how can I leave mother and the children now? Maybe I can get a job in the city by the university while I study and send back all the cash. But each week the savings dwindled, even with her contributions. All the math in the world could not reconcile her calculations. It just didn't add up. No way could it add up.

Chapter 29

The two school-children raced the last mile home after school. The road was lightly iced from the daily sun and the carriage traffic. They followed their noses right up to the back door, sniffing to catch the scent of the fresh-baked cinnamon rolls Mother had promised in the morning. The door flew open, the boots stamped off the extra snow; the coats were unfurled and hung on the hooks. Sniff, sniff. No heavenly smells.

Mother was sitting on her chair, staring at a letter that was propped up against the centerpiece. She was rocking back and forth, wringing her hands, squinting at the return address on the envelope. She didn't even notice the children behind her.

"Mother, what is the matter? You didn't make the sweet rolls."

"Oh, hi, children. What would you like for a snack?"

Johanna looked at Billy, puzzled up her face, and shook her head. "Mother, you promised the cinnamon rolls. Don't you remember?"

"Oh, yeah, sorry, the new postman brought this letter in the mail earlier today."

Ellie had dragged out the family Bible and placed it in front of her chair at the kitchen table. A letter was sitting on top of the Bible.

"What does it say?"

"I didn't open it yet." She looked down at her lap. "...I couldn't open it."

Johanna reached over and picked the letter up. It was addressed to Mrs. Charles Stadler, Centerville, Minnesota. The return address simply said: Backman, RFD, Fargo, ND.

"I couldn't open it, Jo. I don't know anyone in North Dakota. I am scared that it will tell me bad news about Charles. I know Sheriff Braun has contacted the law officers in many cities. I still cling to my hope that Charles will return. I don't think I could go on if he isn't coming back."

When Billy heard his mother talk like that he ran upstairs and slammed his door shut. Mary, over by the fireplace, looked up from her dolls and started whimpering.

"Mother, you have to read it sometime. We have to know what it says."

"You're probably right. But I just can't do it, Jo. Will you read the letter out loud to me?"

Jo wasn't ready to hear bad news either but knew she had to do this.

"O.K., Mother, I'll open it now."

" Please wait a minute while I run up and bring Billy down. We all need to hear this together as a family."

Twenty minutes passed before Ellie brought Billy down to the kitchen. His eyes were red, his nose was running, he was hitting his fist into his baseball glove with each step he took. He came and sat on his mother's right knee. Mary moved to the left one.

Johanna saw that everyone was ready. When she made eye contact with her mother, Ellie nodded nervously.

Johanna torn open the envelope carefully, making sure she preserved the address on the front.

She took a deep breath and unfolded the paper.

"Dear Mrs. Charles Stadler,

I am sorry that I don't remember your given name. I am John Backman and I was Charles' friend from Ohio that moved to Minnesota and convinced you two to move this way, too. I had already moved on over here to Fargo before you arrived in Minnesota But I did receive a couple brief letters from your husband in those early years.

Last week I was in the post office here in Fargo when I noticed a poster from your sheriff asking for any information about the disappearance of Charles Stadler last October. I could not believe what I read. I have not seen Charles. I do not have any clues as to Charles' whereabouts. I wish I could help you more. I wanted to write to see if there was anything I could do to help.

Hopefully, this letter is late, Charles has returned by now and you are having a big sigh of relief reading this.

Please let me know what I can do to help.

.

Sincerely,
John Backman

Johanna looked up at her mother. Confusion, mixed with heartache and anger, twisted Ellie's face. She looked totally deflated. Worn out. Lost.

"That dumb letter don't tell nothing about Father. Nothing but nothing," came out of Billy. He rose from his mother's lap and slowly, clumsily climbed the stairs again.

Mary slipped off her mother's knee and went quickly over to her dolls in the corner. She picked up Daddy Big Doll and placed him up on the seat of the chair, watching over the other dolls.

Jo sat down next to Ellie. "Sorry, Mother. I wish that letter had given us some more hope."

Ellie sat there stone-faced for a long time.

Later, much later after the younger children had both crawled into bed, Ellie looked over at Jo working at her homework. She looked at Jo's back facing her. She knew Jo was crying silently. She could not see the tears but Jo was blowing the tears out of her runny nose. Every half minute a shuddering wave moved her daughter's shoulders up and down.

No one said another word that night. Ellie opened the Bible to the end of Matthew and read her passage again. "I will be with you alway, even unto the end of the world."

Everin C Houkom

Chapter 30

Winter continues

"This is Thursday today. One week ago Emil disappeared," Edith mused as she sat alone in the big, cold farmhouse, looking out at nothing but snowdrifts and bare trees. Her son Emil had left the area without a trace. She still had not heard from him. Calls to his friends' homes turned up no clues. She suspected that her youngest son had headed for Alaska to chase his dreams with his brother Hans Junior. Emil had always been a timid young man, hardly ever saying a word. He had always acted afraid of his loud, explosive father. After Hans Junior left the farm, Emil bore the brunt of her husband's bad temper. Lately he looked like a little puppy that had been beaten too many times. He would crouch down in fear, with his tail between his legs, whenever he was around his father. Unfortunately, he had started stuttering again. He never went to town. In fact he rarely left the farmstead; not until he suddenly disappeared. One week ago he just disappeared. He gave no explanation, only a short good-bye note.

On the other hand, she knew exactly where her husband Hans was most of the time. But she had still lost him, lost him to his bottles of booze. Somehow she felt she had lost him for good this time. He had been a steady drinker several times during

136

their marriage. This last time he had stayed sober for four years. Hans had suddenly begun going to the Duck Blind, a tavern on Main Street that he had basically lived at for years before he had married Edith. Every night he sat at the bar until closing time, often falling asleep right there until the owner Jack woke him and sent him out home. Some nights he never made it home. Edith didn't know where he was on those nights. When he was home, he never answered her questions, just turned his head away or walked over to his chair by the fireplace, a bottle on the table next to him.

Hans began to get into big trouble. He ended up in jail over and over for petty theft or disturbing the peace. Around Thanksgiving he stayed in jail for two weeks. That was when she had first connected with her new friend Ellie, Ellie Stadler. Ellie and she had so much in common these days; both women had lost their husbands this winter. Both women had had beautiful families. Edith's family was gone, now only good memories which were fading away with each week this winter. Ellie's family could have disintegrated also with Charles' disappearance, but they had bonded together and strengthened. They had called up an inner power that had kept them in each other's hearts. The contrast between the two families was huge.

Ever since mid-November Edith basically lived at home alone. She was alone in her house, alone with all the shadows and noises of the wind. The house felt huge without her husband there. She had shut down many parts of the house to conserve on heat but, even so, the rest of the rooms were cavernous. In the dim, evening light, if she caught the tall coat rack in the corner of her eye, she felt it was alive and glaring at her. When she coughed in her chair, the echoes thundered back. The noises from the tree limbs rubbing on the roof would startle her as she was reading. She thought she heard someone in the attic or in the pantry almost every night. She knew it was probably just a mouse or a bat, but in the twilight of her sleep her hopes met up with her fears.

"What would I do without my friendship with Ellie and the children? I feel so wonderful when I am at their house. I am amazed that they are all doing so well without Charles," she often spoke out loud. "The boy Billy has had a tough time without his father. He is doing much better since Christmas. He is becoming a real helper around the house. And Johanna is a special girl. She has been working so hard lately doing extra jobs on the weekend, bringing home some cash for the household. Ellie seems to be ready for the upcoming birth. Little Mary plays with her dolls so contentedly all day. They are so cozy in that little house. But what are they going to do when the baby comes. They really don't have enough room there for another child, especially in a few months when it becomes a toddler. They will live like sardines in a can."

Chapter 31

One bitterly cold night in February, Billie had a revelation.

He began talking to himself in his head. "Mother has been calling me her man of the house. I don't want to believe that Father is gone forever, but now I need to work hard to do as many of the things that Father did here in our family. I bring in the wood each night. And each morning I feed the animals in the barn. When spring arrives, there will be many chores to keep me busy around the yard."

"Tonight I am going to take over the bedtime story-telling for my sister Mary. Father always managed to settle her down each night with a story. I have been reading to her as much as I could but I have not touched the special bedtime books that Father used. Tonight I will ask Mary to choose one of her favorites. Maybe Johanna can be near to help me with any of the big words, at least the first few times."

That night, with the wind whistling through the empty trees, he sat down on the floor next to Mary's bed. Johanna rocked in the chair in the corner.

"Mary, I want to read one of Father's special bed story books for you."

Mary scrunched up her face and looked confused.

Billy saw the worry on Mary's face.

Johanna urged her brother on. Billy had told her his plan earlier when they were finishing the dishes.

Billy continued, "Father read these same stories to me when I was young. But sometimes he would miss a night and Johanna would fill in for him. He told me that that was alright, that the story would still be special even if he was not there that night. Let's try it tonight. You pick the first one for tonight."

Mary was silent for a while then reached over and pulled a book from the shelf. "Okay, this one. "

"That's perfect, Mary. I like this one too."

Billy opened to the first story in the collection. He glanced across the page and knew almost every word he saw. His confidence grew. He cleared his throat and began in his best story-telling voice.

"Once upon a time there was....."

"No, Billy, that is not the way Father did it."

"But that is what is on this page, Mary."

Mary began to pout.

Johanna caught Billy's eye and raised one finger to signal to him to pause a moment.

She turned to Mary and gently asked, "Mary, can you help us tell it just like Father does?"

Mary paused to get herself into her storyteller mood and then began.

"Once upon a time, long before the Indians were in Minnesota and your grandfather was a boy, there was...."

Billy looked confused. Johanna winked at her precious brother.

Johanna sprang forth, "Billy, Father just added some very important words to each story to make them more special. You are both doing so well. Mary, you let Billy start each story from the book and then you help put in the special Father parts when they come and we will have a beautiful story to hear. "

Both children felt big and important after that. Billy was a big, important reader and Mary was the big, important listener who knew the special parts that Father had made up as fathers are want to do. And bedtime story time became the big, important time it had always been.

Chapter 32

March, 1907

Another winter storm was building in the west. Early March was notorious for intense winter storms with copious snow, blizzard winds, white-out conditions and stagnation of all travel in the area. Long before there were weathermen to predict and warn the public, people of the Midwest were experts at reading the signs in the elements.

In the mid-morning, the pure blue sky began to turn to a blue-gray color. There were no billowing clouds, only a gray-washing of the heavens. The warm temperatures of yesterday lingered---not temperatures warm enough to reach the thawing mark, but warm enough to put a melt on the top layer of the sun-washed snow---and continued in the late morning. Now, about eleven, a wet chill was added to the air as the breeze freshened a bit. Blusters of wind sprang up sporadically, rustling the remaining dried oak leaves on the branches. Farmers who were laboring outside felt overdressed that late morning. Coats were opened half-way down the front, exposing the sweat-soaked shirt fronts. Caps were removed. The wind through the tamped-down hair cooled the farmers.

About one o'clock the western horizon sported a few cloud pillows, more dark gray than white. Each minute, the billowing clouds grew higher and higher. The wind increased a little more and the temperature suddenly dropped a few degrees. The coats were buttoned back up halfway. The faces of the farmers contorted in worried looks as the men began to understand the warning signs around them. This could blow itself into a big, mighty, nasty storm. Could it be as massive as the storm of '01, or even '88?

The birds had enjoyed the warm-up yesterday but today they were unsettled. A crow flew straight up and circled above the others, stirring up a frenzy among the flock gathered on the field. Other birds jumped from one tree to another like a bunch of overactive five-year-olds playing in the yard. The choir of crows warmed up their voices in a free form style of music. A raucous melody rose up in the yards. The birds were not quite ready to flee; maybe they knew there was no place where they could escape.

Not to be left out, the animals in the barn also became restless. The chickens scratched in the dirt floor as if there was only one last chance to find the kernels of grain. Cock-fights sprang up here and there. The cattle began to moo their disapproval of the bird noise. The mare, pacing within the confines of the stalls, banged her hooves into the wooden boards. She didn't like the noisy wind, either.

By this time, the weather's angriness had built up mightily. The darkest gray cloud was now matching the darkness of the sky itself. The charcoal clouds were intensifying and piling up and up. In front of all this, streaks of the first snowfall on the western horizon were angled down to the ground. The wind strengthened, and the farmers' coats and hats returned to their totally closed winter state. The farmers knew by now that this was a big storm, no maybe about it. A very big storm.

The teachers at the country school let the students out much earlier than usual that day. Most of the children needed to walk home across country. Only a few of them would have rides from their parents. Since the Great Children's Blizzard of 1888 schools were careful to err on the side of caution and assure that the students did get to safety before a storm blew into the area. In that 1888 storm the blizzard came so quickly in the afternoon that many children were caught walking home in the worst force of the storm. Many hundreds of children were buried and lost that day across the Upper Plains. Everyone in this town knew at least one child who died that day. Better to release the students plenty early, even if the warning signs turned out to be false.

The front door at the Stadler home slammed shut an hour early. Ellie was stoking up the fireplace and turned to see her son stamping the snow off his boots. "Mother, we are in for a great big storm, I think even a blizzard," Billy yelled as he threw down his book bag. "I better run out to the barn and check the animals."

"Oh, Billy, I know about the weather. This unborn baby gave me plenty of clues about that all day. This is not the kind of day to be outside by yourself. Make sure that you and Johanna go out to the barn together today. She can help you with the barn chores and then you can help a little here inside." Ellie was about to add that she didn't want to lose another from the family but stopped herself in time. No need to bring up thoughts of Charles today. We are all doing so amazingly well these months and we will need all our faculties today.

Indeed, Charlie/Charlotte had kicked a constant warning to her that day. Even before the sky started to turn gray, Ellie had felt extra movement in her womb. "This child kicks more than a galloping horse," she thought. The baby had sensed the change in the air pressure. Actually, it probably sensed the tightening of Ellie's womb around it. Give me more room, Mother, I need more room it kicked in Morse code. All day the baby had tumbled around. In fact, Ellie was quite sore. Twice before the children arrived home from school she thought that the uterine tightenings were getting almost regular, a very disturbing possibility.

"Don't even think about coming into this world today, baby. You need to stay safe in there at least until April." The baby must have listened to mother as the gymnastics settled down just before the children arrived home. Ellie had gone into the bathroom and checked; no leaking of fluid, no show. I think I am safe.

Billy and Jo went out and took care of the barn and animals while Ellie minded the kettle of soup on the stove. She made a fresh batch of biscuits as well. She had baked an apple cobbler with the last of the fall apples from the cellar to surprise the children. Mary had been sworn to secrecy about the dessert and Ellie had the pan hidden away out of sight. The bread smells were so strong that the sweet apple aroma was undetected in the air. Ellie wanted some comfort food for the family during this storm. She sensed that they were in for a long confinement at the farm. This stacked up to be a big blizzard.

Out in the barn, chores went quickly with two pairs of hands. Back inside, as Billy and Johanna were removing their parkas and boots, the whole family heard a terrible tearing sound outside as a huge branch of the tree out front fell across the pathway. The wind had picked up even in the short time since they had arrived home from school. Jo felt an extra jolt as she pictured Billy and herself right there just one minute before.

Supper was fun. The food was a big hit. The cobbler was perfect. Jo and Billy settled in at the sink to clean up the dishes, guessing at how much snow would be out there by the time the storm ended. Both of them picked a remaining branch of the front yard tree to mark the top of the predicted snow bank.

Next Jo and Billy settled down at the table to do the school work that they had brought home. Anticipating a few homebound days, the teachers had supplied enough assignments to last three or four days but Billy wanted to finish tonight so he would have no worries the rest of his free time. Johanna smiled at his enthusiasm. *I was like that at his age. When he finishes his work assignments I can challenge him with some great problems and mind-twisters. I'll keep him busy.*

Ellie sat down in her chair by the fire and relaxed. Putting her swollen feet up on the stool felt so good after the long day. She looked over and caught a glimpse of Johanna and Billy at the table head to head and dreamed again the recurring memory of her husband there with Jo. *I miss him so much. Maybe he will blow in on the wind and land in the snow bank like a snow fairy. I so wish he could be here for this child's birth.* Mary came over and asked her mother to read the story about Baby Jesus that they heard on Christmas. The heavy heirloom Bible came out and all the family took a few minutes to listen to Ellie read the words.

As everyone predicted at the Stadler home, the storm was a whopper. Two days later, when the winds blew themselves out, three feet of new snow blanketed the ground. The snowdrifts were much taller than the predictions of both Billy and Johanna. The drift between the house and the barn towered so high they could not see the top of the barn door. The family was cozy in the house; there was still plenty of wood for the fireplace and stove. Ellie's womb had settled down and the baby was tucked quietly where it belonged. Only one negative--- Charles had not appeared in the white magic.

Chapter 33

.

.

A gorgeous day here in the Minnesota woodlands. Ellie and Mary had decided to go for a walk along the path to meet Charles at the river crossing. The ground was covered with the fallen leaves of the sugar maples and red maples and the huge leaves of the basswood. This made the path surprisingly slippery. The loose leaves moved under their shoes; the rains yesterday had created a muddy layer. Mary found several wet spots, even some puddles, inviting her to jump and splash. Of course. What child would pass up the chance to get her shoes wet?

"Is Daddy coming soon, Mother? I can't see him across the river. "

"We are almost up to the spot where your father crosses the water. You will see a big log spanning the water. It blew down in the big storm last year and now is a place where a grown-up like your father can scoot across high above the water. We can just watch though, it is way too dangerous for us."

"Okay, Mother. I will just watch. I don't want to go across the water."

Just then Ellie heard some frantic yelling in the woods ahead. Mary grabbed her mother's hand tightly. It sounded like Charles' voice. He sounded like he is in big trouble.

"Charles, we are coming. What's wrong, darling?"

Quickly Ellie and Mary reached the small clearing by the crossing. Now Ellie could quickly assess the trouble. Charles was on the other side of the river and was running up to the log at full speed. A bear was chasing right behind, almost at his heels. A pack of wolves followed right behind the bear. Charles jumped up unto the log and began to run across. No scooting on his seat. Right from the start he was out of balance. His arms were flailing and circling, trying to maintain control. The bear had run off into the forest safety *as soon as it saw Ellie. The wolves clustered on the opposite bank and barked their disappointment at Charles' escape* out of their reach.

Where was Mary? Ellie turned around briefly to locate her daughter. Luckily, Mary had returned to the woods, gathering up pretty leaves for her collection. She was looking away from the river. Good! She doesn't need to see her father right now.

Turning her attention back to the river, Ellie saw that Charles was not doing well on the log. He was balancing on one leg, leaning over the water. Once he saw Ellie holding out her hand for him to grab he seemed to calm down slightly and slow down his movements. He took two more steps over toward her on the log bridge and reached out his arm. But the shift in weight caused the log to roll a bit and he lost all the control he had just gained. For just an instant he looked lovingly into Ellie's eyes. His nose began to melt away into watery ooze and drip off his face. Then his right eye, his right ear, even his blond hair, all dripped away. He was slipping away from her; he was dripping away from her. Huge drops of his face and now his neck and shoulders were falling to the river below, joining the rushing current. She could see the flesh-colored water in the river for just seconds. She was losing him. Charles was disappearing. Now she could not recognize his face at all.

Ellie's stomach revolted with the fear. She doubled over, clutching her abdomen. I can't do anything. I can't help him. I am losing him forever….. He is almost gone.

·—

Now Mary is grabbing on to her mother's legs frantically. The branches of the river bank bushes are tangled around Ellie's hips and she cannot move forward.

"Mommy, Mommy," she hears as she wakes up. "Mommy, what is wrong? Are you Okay? You were crying and yelling so loud, Mommy. "

Now Ellie was fully awake. Her legs were wrapped up in the blankets and Mary was next to the bed, pulling on her ankles. Her uterus was tight and tense, squeezing the baby inside.

Those last frightening views of her husband lingered in her memory. I can't recognize him. I can't remember what his face was like. I honestly can't picture my husband's loving face. Charles was dripping away. I am losing him, I am losing him forever. A moment later, she speaks dejectedly-—"I have lost him." She cannot call up his facial features anymore. "He is gone."

After a few minutes her uterus thankfully relaxed and no regular labor began. Ellie looked out the window. Nothing but white snow blanketed everywhere. No variation in the white, just blurry white. Just like her last dream picture of Charles.

Chapter 34

April, 1907

That huge storm in early March was the last significant snow of the season. The drifts were still everywhere in the yards and along the sides of the roads but the bright afternoon sun was melting them down, consolidating them into shiny, dense snowpack. The drifts around the house created inches of water in the pathway, a fact that Billy and Mary and their boots loved. The daylight was extending on each end of the day as well. Another two or three minutes of light each day did wonders for the spirits of everyone.

Ellie felt her baby move all the time now. Some days she would think that her labor was beginning only to feel the rhythm break after a couple hours. She and Edith had a plan now for the delivery. Edith was able to get over to the house with her carriage or sleigh at will now. The women had contacted one of the neighbor ladies, Mrs. Bernhardt, who functioned as a midwife for the German families out there in the country and she was happy to be on call for the delivery. Here was plan A.

When Ellie gave the word, Johanna planned to run over to the Schultz family and use the phone to call Edith and then rush home again to be with her mother. Edith would call the doctor in town, pick up her already-packed overnight suitcase and drive over to the Stadler home, gathering Mrs. Bernhardt along the way. Ellie was not going to chance the roads at all while in labor. Her last labor had lasted only about four hours, and she had not had all these pre-term labor episodes then. This labor might go surprisingly fast. Delivering in the snow bank between home and nowhere was not a smart option. Johanna stayed home from school these days, having arranged a schedule of assignments with her teachers. She was in no danger of flunking her last year. She was motivated to be the best student possible. Billy also stayed home since he had no way to get over to school without his sister. Occasionally one of the neighbor fathers would stop by the Stadler home on the way to the schoolhouse and pick him up. Billy was excited to go to see all his friends but, at the same time, was worried he would miss the birth of his new brother. He just *knew* it was a boy. Another girl in the family would not be fair. This was Charles Junior.

The first week of April arrived without incident. Ellie had felt regular contractions off and on the previous day. She noticed some show on her underwear when she went to bed that night. The doctor and midwife had calculated the date of confinement as April 25th. I don't know if this young one is going to wait that long to poke a nose out into the world, she thought to herself. "You have a notion to come early, don't you, little one. I think it is time for plan B."

Plan B was to have Edith come and stay there at the house, ready to help immediately. The children could periodically go to school that way and yet all would be ready for a quick delivery. If Johanna was not at home, Edith could easily get over to the nearest neighbor's house in just a few minutes to alert them and they were poised to call the doctor in town and rush over to get Mrs. Bernhardt. Edith would return to the house immediately. This would put Edith at Ellie's side as much as possible. Edith, in fact, had attended several deliveries herself over the years. She did not call herself a midwife but knew what to do nonetheless. Most rural women in the Midwest at the turn of the century knew these skills. The men worked the cattle; the women took care of each other.

Edith expelled a big sigh of relief the evening that Johanna had arrived to ask her to come and stay at the house. She felt much better with plan B. She buttoned up the stove, made sure all the windows were closed and latched, grabbed her bag and was ready in a flash.

"Let's go, young lady. I am so ready for this. I have been sitting on pins and needles this past week. I will follow you so we will have both of the carriages at your house. "

Like clockwork the labor began the next day. The family had just finished breakfast when Ellie let out a big shriek followed by a long peal of laughter. She lifted out of her chair and looked at the huge puddle of fluid surrounding her space.

"Here we go, everyone, here we go. Baby is coming today."

Johanna left immediately for the neighbor's house to start Plan B and flew back in time to be with her mother for the birth. Johanna had missed the birth of Mary almost five years ago."I cannot miss this one," she thought. Billy was along in the carriage so he was out of the way of the busy women. It didn't matter what age a male was, he was not much help with this birth thing.

In perfect order, all the women were present at the time of delivery. Ellie had been right in her instincts; after not quite three hours she was pushing out a beautiful head of blonde hair. Johanna instinctively knew what to do as her mother's attendant, at Ellie's side, providing support and encouragement. Edith and Mrs. Bernhardt sat back and let the miracle happen. No grabbing onto the baby or pulling. They wisely let the delivery progress without interference. This process had been going on for thousands of years and had a natural way. The doctor drove into the yard just as the crowning occurred, hearing the final pushes and the first natal cry as he rushed up the steps. Billy and Mary flew down the stairs from their bedrooms when they heard the baby cries, not waiting for Edith's signal to come down. Mrs. Gerhardt stepped forward at the last to catch the slippery infant, wrap it warm blankets, and hand the bundle carefully up to mother.

Ellie peeked at the beautiful baby, inspecting its bottom last.

"Billy, Mary, Johanna, Edith, Gisele, oh,-- and Doctor, this is our new son."

Billy piped up, "His name is Charles, just like my Daddy's name."

Charles was not here. But little Charles had arrived. The baby's vigorous crying quickly overwhelmed them all. Each took a turn at holding the bundle of blankets and arms and legs. Each took a turn at looking straight into the eyes and soul of this new person, this lovely beautiful boy. Johanna's heart melted immediately and her anger and resentment at her father hid away behind her love for her new brother. Billy brought out his baseball glove and told his new brother the story of Uncle William and Billy's father Charles and Billy Named-after-Uncle-William and Baby-Charles-Named-after-Father. Mary brought over a special doll she had saved to give to her little "sister." (For four-year-old Mary, all babies were little girls, of course).

Ellie gazed at her infant son's face contentedly. "He has his father's nose and mouth---- and he got his father's straw-colored hair. Hello Charles, I love you."

Chapter 35

Edith stayed over at the Stadler home for almost three weeks after the birth. Each night, the couch was decked out with a thin mattress and several cozy blankets. Lying close to the fireplace, Edith was able to stoke the fire at least one extra time each night to keep the house nice and warm for the newborn. Mary's bed was moved down to the front room right next to Aunt Edith's couch from its place next to Ellie's bed. (She had been sleeping close to her mother ever since Father had disappeared.) The cradle took its place right beside mother's bed, close for rocking and breast-feeding. Billy began to sort through his toys in his room so there would be room for Baby Charles' bed when he was old enough.

Johanna and Billy returned to the routine of school attendance. Joseph and Andrew, and Henry especially, clung to Billy each day, afraid that he might disappear again. They had missed him so much. The stories poured out of them as they brought Billy up to date on all the things he missed, like the time Joseph put a snake on Karen's desk or the time the three of them had put glue in Amy Nelson's boots. Billy brought the baseball glove to school even though he had shared it at show-and-tell last fall when his grandfather had told him about his Uncle

William. But now the story of his little brother was woven into the fabric of that leather glove and he needed it as a prop as he told the birth story of little Charles. Little Charles Named-after-Father.

Johanna's return to the classroom reminded her of how much she loved sharing learning with others. Her sessions with Billy at home had been precious but they could not take the place of her time with her teacher and the other upper grade students. She had kept up with the work easily enough but her advanced communication skills were a bit rusty. April was just two months away from graduation.

Miss Block let Johanna go into town to the new Carnegie Library on two consecutive Fridays. She asked Johanna to prepare a special lesson for all the other students about architecture. Johanna would never forget the first time she entered the new building and saw all the woodwork and the rows and rows of bookshelves. The town had been so fortunate that Mr. Carnegie from Pittsburgh, Pennsylvania had funded the library. Mr. Carnegie had first endowed only libraries close to his Pittsburgh home. In fact,. almost every town or village in Pennsylvania had been gifted with a new building. Just when he decided to branch out his philanthropy into other states the shirt-tail Carnegies in Centerville sent him a letter reminding him of their shared bloodline. Could he fund a library in Minnesota? It would be such an honor to have the family name on such an important building in Centerville. He could hardly refuse his favorite Aunt Willamina's daughter. Since the citizens of Centerville did not need to contribute a cent to the library building, the local Carnegies were able to raise a substantial sum to supply the large collection of books to put on the massive shelves.

Johanna found the architecture shelf for her school project. It wasn't long before her wandering eyes discovered the enormous fiction section. What a wonder! All these exciting stories were here so close to her home. She soon left the architecture books on the table and leafed through some of the classic novels. Reading the prose of Charles Dickens was like traveling to England itself. Edgar Allen Poe was a masterful story-teller; the House of the Seven Gables intrigued her no end. Of course she had to borrow those books as well as the drafting and engineering texts to complete her school presentation. She struggled to carry the book bag to the carriage until two young men rushed over from the feed store and fought over it. Jo smiled nervously but felt a funny flush in her face as she climbed into the carriage.

Ellie concentrated on catching up on her rest. Aunt Edith entertained Mary during the day and took over the cooking for the family. Mary truly enjoyed learning how to prepare the new foods that Aunt Edith chose. Cutting up the carrots and turnips and potatoes for soup was her favorite task. She was very careful with the sharp knife. Of course, she also spent plenty of time "taking care" of the new baby. She would fetch the diapers and sleepers from the drawer, always remembering the little socks for the tiny cold feet of her "sister." Of course Mary knew little Charles was a boy but she still called him her sister. Ellie never slipped into the baby blues like she had with her other babies. She missed her husband so much, but little Charles lifted her spirits each time she pondered his face.

Edith loved the chance to be needed again. She had been so lonely in that big house where she had raised her boys. It had been way too large for her sitting alone there all winter. She missed her son Emil. She had still not heard anything from him since he left home before Thanksgiving. Her husband Hans was now in the state prison one hundred and fifty miles away in St. Paul; each release from the jail had been followed with another drinking binge and more trouble with the law. Edith had even gone down to see Hans once last month. Sheriff Braun accompanied her on the train since he was attending a statewide meeting there anyway. She was with Hans for thirty long minutes. Her husband had not once spoken to her. He stared at the wall behind her and closed his eyes for most of the one way conversation. There was no physical contact, not even a stiff hug. Edith had cried most of the way back to Centerville. Sheriff Braun had been so supportive and a great listener.

One big thing was welling up in Edith these days. She saw

how tiny the Stadler home was, especially with the new baby. The family was crammed into the space like a full sack of potatoes. There was no room to turn around. What would it be like when the baby became a toddler, cruising around the rooms looking for new trouble at each step? "Maybe I can help. Maybe we should exchange houses. This little place here would be perfect for me alone. And if Hans ever did return home we would still have enough room in the Stadler house. Our large house and the big yard and garden out back would work perfectly for the Stadlers. Let's see if I can make that happen this summer."

Johanna also knew how precarious the family was here at the farmhouse. She knew how close to the bottom of the bin she reached when fetching the potatoes and other vegetables. She also knew that her mother's bank account was almost gone too. Her small jobs on the weekends had squeaked them through the winter. But there was no other income coming into the budget. Her father had provided for them as a mailman but Mother had always stayed home to take care of the household. Now there was no money coming from the post office. What will happen when I leave for college? Will I be able to leave for college? Oh, my goodness, what can we do?

Thankfully, the stream of neighbors started up again as the weather permitted travel. The housewives that had rallied around the Stadlers when Charles disappeared saw the new baby and the new challenges for the family and the suppers and breads and preserves flowed in again. One farmer brought over meat from a freshly-slaughtered hog. Three new hens were out in the barn joining the dwindling flock. But Johanna knew in her heart that this bounty would not last forever. "Oh, my goodness, what should I do?"

Chapter 36

Pastor Jorstad and Sheriff Braun hatched the same idea independently and simultaneously. They met at the coffee shop on a bright spring morning.

Pastor Jorstad began, "John, I want to bounce an idea off of you. I believe I have a good job for dear Johanna Stadler, a job that will exercise that young intellect and provide the family some much needed income. She wants to attend college next year but I am afraid that she will have to put that dream aside for a while."

John Braun chuckled, his index finger pointed at his brain, and replied, "Pastor, you are not thinking of the library position, are you? "

John had been puzzling over this question for several weeks. Lydia Williams, the eighty-year-old librarian, had died suddenly after a serious accident. The new Carnegie library needed a dedicated smart librarian to bring out the best in this incredible gift.

"How did you know? They say great minds think alike," Pastor laughed. "Doesn't this coincidence point to a masterful perfection in our scheme? How could it go wrong?"

"Yes, it does. Edith Hanson has spoken with me about the

poor family and I've had discussions with her about what we can do for the Stadlers. I do not know how the family has done so well since Charles disappeared. The strength of love and friendship must be so strong. Most families around here would have fallen completely apart by now."

"Don't forget the power of prayer, Sheriff. A day has not gone by that I have not mentioned them in my prayers."

Sheriff was not a churchgoer himself, but he had to admit to himself that he had been "speaking to heaven" about Ellie and the children as well.

John continued, "I am relieved that they are doing so well emotionally. I paid a visit to them last week. They seem to be thriving, what with that new son Charles Junior in their midst. But the grocers and feed store owners will not accept promises and smiles and thank-yous much longer. An income needs to appear soon for that household. I know that Johanna has been dreaming about college for several years. But I can't imagine that she can go off to the big city just yet. She is the only one who could possibly replace the income that Charles was bringing home. The library job would go a long way to accomplish that."

"So right, John. Selling her on the idea will be the hard part. First I will speak to Edith as soon as I can. That woman is actually part of the family now, practically living there with them. I know that Johanna adores her 'Aunt Edith.' Having a co-

conspirator in the house will not hurt."

"Good. I believe that the bond that Edith has felt with Ellie and the children has undoubtedly saved her as well. God knows she hasn't had any support from that husband Hans. Now he is stuck in that prison for at least another year. And with no hope of clemency, not the way he carries on there in the cell."

"Can you speak about this at the library board meeting tonight, John?"

"You bet. Finally something new and important to discuss. All those years of sitting through abominable monthly meetings surely has given me some credentials with the group. Johanna's high school teacher, Miss Block, is on the board as well. I suspect she will speak up for her prize student wholeheartedly."

Their conversation drifted to other town topics. It wasn't gossip exactly. More like concerns about their neighbors. This growing town had plenty of problems to keep the town fathers busy: new businesses and an expanding presence of the railroad to name two big things. Sheriff Braun needed to focus on town security. Questions abounded. Does this town need another deputy, another jail cell? How can he work with the train security effectively? Can the town council corral the bars and saloons into one area to better police them? But today none of those concerns outweighed the concern he had for the Stadlers. Families like that should continue to form the backbone of our town.

Pastor Jorstad also had many other things on his mind. He was privy to many secret worries and battles in the lives of his parishioners. Life was so difficult for many of them. Too often circumstances out of their control bludgeoned the folks into despair. He had so many prayers to keep in mind.

He also knew that Edith had hatched an idea to help the Stadlers even more. He thought it was a good plan. "I hope Hans will agree when Edith talks about this house exchange with him. I will go with her to the prison next week so I can help influence him when she springs the master plan. A train ride out of town will do me good. A short break after a long winter will feel delightful."

Chapter 37

The next Wednesday, Edith and Pastor Jorstad climbed on the train and settled in for the trip down to the state prison. Not ten minutes had gone by before Pastor was snoring away in his seat by the aisle. Edith did not mind. She had lived with a thunderous snorer her whole married life. Her husband Hans' snoring had always been soothing to her, believe it or not. She knew that, at least while he was snoring, he could not be giving her negative arguments about her ideas. He rarely agreed with her when he was awake. Everything had to be his way; every idea had to be his idea.

"Not today, Hans," she thought. "Today you will listen to my plan. It is a good plan and you will pay attention this time..... Dear God, help me today."

Soon a change in the rhythm of the train signaled that the big city was upon them. A couple lurches and plenty of squeals gave all the passengers a chance to wake up from their slumbers. Yes, even Edith had succumbed to the sleep genie. In fact, her snores were just as loud as those in the aisle seat but of a sweeter, higher pitch. A bubble of anxiety settled in the center of her gut as she woke up to her surroundings. She could feel her pounding pulse in her temples. A series of long, deep breaths calmed her down. They exited the train.

A short hansom cab ride brought them to the entrance of the prison. They were expected---her letters had set everything up. The warden was very nice. He wasn't sure if Hans would have anything to say but he assured Edith that the guards would bring them together in a safe way so she could have a discussion with her husband.

"Our officers will be just out of earshot, ready to spring over to you if needed. I hope you can get Mr. Hanson to speak at least a few words. Silence is not a good companion for an inmate. He has been shrinking inside himself more and more. Be prepared, Mrs. Hanson, you may not recognize the skinny carcass you will encounter."

Even with the warning from the warden, Edith was shocked when she saw Hans sitting in the chair by the far wall of the community room. She noted the two guards across the room, each nodding to her encouragingly as she approached her life mate. She also saw the cockroach scurrying along the baseboards and the cobweb up in the far corner of the room.

"Hello, Hans." She sat down straight across from her husband. The hard, straight-backed chair added to her discomfort. Hans sat motionless--- with no eye contact. The skin on his neck hung loosely. He looked pale, almost pasty.

"Hans, please listen to me just this one time." She waited for a response. Hearing nothing, she continued, "I will continue to speak to you even if you don't answer. I need to discuss a plan I have with you. "

He shrunk deeper into his chair. He kept staring at the wall behind her head.

"Hans, I want to do something for our neighbors, the Stadlers. You remember they lost Charles last fall---he up and vanished. He has still not surfaced. His wife Ellie had a baby last month, a beautiful baby boy. I have stayed with the family for several weeks to help. Their house is so small--- way too small for the expanding family. And our house is so huge now that you and Emil are gone. The air blows around in there like the north wind. Some nights the echoes are deafening, only quieting when I sing myself to sleep. I still hope that you will be able to return some day to me. I still love you, Hans. But even when you come back, the Stadler home would be a perfect size for the two of us. So here is my plan. I want to exchange our houses. We will live in the small Stadler home and they will move over into our big place. Please, Hans, tell me you will agree. Please look at me and say something."

Edith knew Hans was listening; his icy gaze had darted over to her face with her first words. Then a scowl had formed, his eyebrows piled up above his eyes. He was drumming his fingers on the table while she presented her plan but by the time she was done talking, he was still again.

Eternity passed by as Edith waited. Then a squirming in Hans chair gave her hope. Finally, her husband mumbled a few sounds, maybe words.

"Sorry, Hans, I couldn't hear you. Please repeat that for me."

Talking to the back of his hand, Hans yelled out, "Do whatever you want with that house. I don't want anything to do with that place. Just leave me alone. I don't care about the house, I tell you. I will never go back there."

The guards had responded quickly to his raised voice and had jumped across the room to the couple. Edith looked up at them and smiled, motioning them back again. Hans will surely clam up if they come closer, she thought. The men moved back to their stations.

"Hans, are you sure about the house? I need a signature on this paper for the bank. Will you sign?"

Hans grabbed the paper and the pen and scribbled a scrawling mark across the open space at the bottom.

Again he raised his voice, "There, good riddance to that place. I'm never coming back to Centerville. Never."

Edith could not believe that he could say such things. Didn't he remember the day he carried her over the threshold? Didn't he remember all the memories of the boys growing up there? Didn't he remember the barn raising party the second summer they were there, all the neighbors coming to help and celebrate? The many Christmases and anniversaries and birthdays?

She was about to ask him these questions but he had sunk

into his chair even deeper than before and turned his back to her. She wanted to give him just one simple hug but he waved her away as she approached. Dismissed her from his life. His eyes closed tightly, his shoulders scrunched closed. She turned and walked out to the lobby where Pastor Jorstad was waiting, waiting with the fatherly hug she needed and the shoulder to cry on.

"I still love him, I do, Pastor." Through the sobs, she managed to say, "Let's go, I am exhausted."

Chapter 38

End of April 1907

Spring had arrived.

The snow banks were melting; a trapezoid of ground poked out on the crest of the front yard. Birds were in the treetops, flitting about, looking for bare ground. They fought madly for the right to dig in that bare earth for the tidbits of interest. The shortest birds won the most, hopping under the breasts of the crows and pigeons. An eagle surveyed the ground from his tree-top perch. Moles and voles and rabbits, look out! I am hungry! I will find you!

The path to the barn was covered with three inches of melt water. Billy enjoyed scooting his boots through the water, watching the waves hit the side drifts of snow. He also loved to open the barn doors and let the spring air in for the captive animals. As soon as the sunlight beamed in, these domestics protested their confinement, resenting having to stay inside on such sunny days. Billy was able to lead the mare and Aunt Edith's horse out to the sand oasis in front of the barn. Even though the outside space to roam was only slightly larger than the stalls, the mares acted like they were free in a broad field of clover. Billy brushed the coats of the team and felt the smooth hair on his palms. Soon he would be working in the garden, working the tasks that his father always relished in the weeks after winter.

In the house, Ellie and the other females were also feeling frisky. The side windows were forced open and the breeze played through the rooms. The fresh flow whisked the stale winter air away.

"Be careful with that draft on Baby Charles. Cover his head loosely, Johanna."

"Oh, Mother, he wants to have a little of this heaven as well. I will be careful." Johanna bent down and lifted the blanket, adoring the smooth skin and silky hair of the sleeping boy.

With the liberation of spring, thoughts of Charles resurfaced strongly in Ellie. Every other spring, he had been outside from the time he got home until after dark, finding projects to keep him busy. He could usually be dragged in for a quick supper with the family but Ellie never expected to see him again before bedtime. He would come in finally just in time for the bedtime stories and a conversation with Johanna about her schoolwork. In the spring, Charles was betrothed to the outside.

Ellie missed Charles so much it hurt. His disappearance was still the biggest mystery of the winter. Sheriff Braun had come out to the farmstead shortly after the birth of Baby Charles. He didn't have any new information or theories. He asked if any new insights had come to the family.

Ellie speculated, "Charles either went into the river or deep in the quicksand of Riley's Bog. Those are the only options. I still can't believe he would have just walked out on us."

"The roads and path by the river are still much too wet to traverse this spring but Deputy Coffey and I will get out there as soon as we are able to recheck for clues. We will try to re-trace Charles steps from that day once more. I doubt we will find any clues, but of course, we will give it another try."

Sheriff left the house feeling terrible. There was just nothing more to say to Ellie Stadler. It had been a short visit. He did remind himself that he needed to spend some time with Billy, some man time.

Spring also brought more worries about the family finances. Ellie's heart hurt each time she thought of Johanna and the future. She found herself arguing with herself, college or work, education or experience, poverty or money. Could Ellie find a way to bring in the cash? No, her oldest daughter was the only person who could bring home a sufficient income.

"I wish Jo could go off to college and study for her dream vocation. But I cannot let her leave. The bank teller told me last week we have spent down our savings to less than fifty dollars. Our vegetables are gone. We can't expect the neighbors to bring all their food gifts forever either. We have been so blessed by them. How do I have the talk with Johanna?"

Ellie didn't need to bring this up with Johanna. That very night Jo started the talk with her mother. She finished the dishes and kitchen clean-up, scurried Mary and Billy up to bed, listened to a chapter of the Billy's bedtime story with them and then turned out their bedroom lights. As she descended the stairs, she called to her mother.

"Can we sit down at the table and have a talk, Mother?"

Positioning her mother on the chair nearest the fireplace, Johanna paused, took a deep breath, straightened her posture and, as if giving an important speech, she began.

"Mother, I want to find a job in town. During the summer and fall, I can easily drive the carriage myself and still live here at home. In the winter months, I can find a room in one of the boarding houses on Main Street. Edith and I have already discussed the plan for her to loan me her spare team and rig so that you and Billy will have a way to get help if you need it during the day. A job will build up the family bank account quickly. I have an amazing opportunity. Pastor Jorstad and Sheriff Braun have approached me about the city librarian job. The library board has met and wants to offer me the job. My teacher feels that I can easily handle that job--- and I love books. I have fallen in love with the new Carnegie Library. It would be an honor to continue to build that library into the treasure it could be for our town."

"Oh, Johanna. What about your dreams of being an engineer or mathematician? How about college? Even though you and your father have tried to keep me in the dark about those ideas I know those are your dreams."

"Mother, if the world was perfect and we hadn't lost Father last fall, I would be planning for college this very minute. But the world is not perfect. We need to make good with what we have. A job in the library can allow me to be a *people* architect and build the children of Centerville into the best they can be, to mold them into important citizens and future leaders. I already have visions of the great things I can do here in our little town. Mother, please permit me to say yes to this opportunity. It truly is what I want to do. It is my new calling. I have spoken to Edith and Pastor Jorstad about this, too, and they both agree that this feels like a calling from God. Like He spoke to Moses and Elijah. I have been reading the story of Moses in the Bible and he argued and argued with God when he was called. But then he relented and said, 'Here I am, Lord.' That's how I feel."

"Oh, Johanna, dear, I love you so much. You are so like your father. All right, you have my blessing."

Hugs, smiles, kisses and a few tears mixed as the two women shared this moment.

Ellie thought to herself, "Charles is still looking after us here. He helped raise this amazing young woman. I am so proud of her. Maybe we can get Jo to college in a year or so. "

Chapter 39

Johanna drove into town straight from school the next day. Billy rode along but as soon as the carriage hit Main Street he was off and running to the general store to find some penny candy. Jo had given him a dime and his instructions included buying treats for his little sister as well.

Johanna presented herself to the library where one of the elderly town women was trying to keep the place running. Pastor Jorstad and the president of the library board were to meet her there in a few minutes. Johanna wandered through the stacks, first gravitating to the math and science collection but soon distracted by the large fiction section. She had been in the library plenty of times for her school project. But now her presence here felt different. This was to be her domain, her responsibility. Just touching the spines of these books gave her a spark in her chest and a chill down her spine.

The meeting went quickly. The library board had heard from Pastor and from Johanna's teacher last week. They wanted to give this home-grown girl every opportunity at this position. They also recognized the chance to save some money on salary by hiring someone without formal experience. The committee had also approached the school board last week about collaboration. The high school was without a librarian right now and the city librarian job description now included two days a week over at the high school. All the library board members had shown up for this meeting. They all wanted to meet this young woman from Centerville. The Carnegie niece nodded her approval as she heard Johanna speak and present her new ideas. As the meeting wrapped up Johanna realized she had never shaken the hand of a man before. The firm grip of the board president felt so grown-up, so mature. That firmness gave Jo a feeling of confidence, a feeling of accomplishment. She stood up straighter, meeting the man eye-to-eye.

"Thank you so much for this opportunity to serve Centerville. I think my parents have prepared me well for this chance. And Miss Block has been amazing. I can start full-time as soon as school is finished. My instructors even told me that I could come into town on Fridays starting this week to learn the basic tasks here from the volunteers. I have actually finished the school work I need to graduate."

"Great, Miss Stadler. This job feels like it was designed exactly for someone like you. Welcome to our Centerville team. We look forward to working with you." Turning to the full board, the president announced, "It is my privilege to present to you our new city librarian, Johanna Stadler."

As she left the library, rounded up Billy from the store, and drove out of town she could hear the pleasing sound of "Miss

Stadler" in her head. The old mare knew the way home and she let Billy take over the reins. Jo's head was in the clouds.

Chapter 40

The big day of the house exchange had arrived. Many of the neighbors were in the yard, ready to grab the Stadler household belongings piece by piece and haul them over across the river to Edith Hanson's place. A festive feeling permeated the crowd. Virtually everyone west of Centerville had arrived to pitch in to the project. They had lined their carriages along the narrow driveway. The husbands brought in the empty wooden boxes they had brought from home and immediately the house wares began to be packed carefully. Mary and Billy were jumping up and down every time another load came out of the house. Each "supervised" the transfer of their own important belongings. In no time, the Stadler possessions were stacked on the many carriages and the long procession of teams moved over to Edith's house. One of the farmers began belting out *Amazing Grace* in his Swedish brogue and soon the whole procession chimed in. Other songs followed. The singing echoed as they crossed the river. Once they arrived at the Hanson home, off came the boxes and furniture, the drawers full of clothes and toys. The kitchen pots banged against each other like the percussion in a marching band. The neighbor wives brought their food creations down for the party afterward. Three long tables appeared in the front yard for the feast.

All the Stadler items were unpacked and Edith's things loaded up. Later, Edith's belongings were to be transported back to the smaller Stadler house. Much of Edith's furniture would be left in the big house for the new family. The moving crew went right to work, eying the tables of food as they carried Edith's household across the yard.

Edith's favorite rocking chair was moving with her, of course. Most of the needlework she produced in her years of marriage had been created in that chair. Joseph Train approached the rocking chair, sat down in the plush seat and jumped up howling and pulling a stray needle out of his backside. Plenty of jokes about that enormous backside followed with the laughter erupting all around. "Surprised we didn't hear a big hiss of air, Joseph----thought that was where you kept all your hot air." Joseph laughed the loudest. For his trouble, Edith brought him the biggest piece of her special coffee cake. Joseph searched each of the other chairs, looking for another sewing sharpie, secretly hoping for another big piece of gastronomic paradise.

Joseph's backside was to be the only casualty of the event. By three in the afternoon the house packing was complete and the festivities began. Picnickers formed in long lines, eying all the amazing food. Goose Johnson brought out his fiddle, Kenny, his brother, strung up a string bass and Joe Barry Olson exercised his voice with some vigorous calling. Three squares formed quickly and the children flowed around the dancers, mimicking the elders as they learned new steps and moves.

Sally Olsen, one of the girls in Billy's school class, approached Henry's mother, both hands coyly joined behind her back and a big smile on her face. Mrs. Carlson bent down to speak with her and soon took Sally's right hand and headed straight for her son Henry and the other boys. She grabbed Henry by his shoulders and coaxed him up face-to-face with Sally and took his left hand and placed it gently on Sally's right shoulder. Next she made Henry hold hands and pushed the couple out in to the dance area. His lucky friends hooted and hollered at Henry, laughing at his plight and their good fortune.

Billy noticed his mother watching him in the gang of taunting boys. "Is she coming over for me?" he wondered. Quick as a jackrabbit, Billy ran to the side of the barn and found an empty wooden basket. Just as quickly, he ran back to the musicians, turned the basket upside down, and sat down on top. His hands began to beat out the rhythm of the dance and he put on a look of "look at me. I'm too important for the music to be dancing with a girl." Ellie smiled and let him have his moment.

Sheriff Braun approached Ellie and asked for a dance. Hesitantly, she assented and soon showed a smile of relaxation---and fun. Pastor Jorstad butted in on the second song and before she knew what happened she had filled her dance card with all the neighbor men's requests.

But Ellie was only the second Stadler woman to fill her card. As soon as the work of moving was finished Johanna had been surrounded by a large circle of hopeful young gents. Gerhardt Schultz, Rolly Olson, and Henry Anderson were especially persistent.

After his second turn dancing with Johanna, Rolly Olson tried his hardest to sneak a kiss from Johanna. But his peck on her cheek missed and his lips stuck out into the air like a largemouth bass. Joseph Train, still rubbing his backside, immediately saw his chance to transfer attention to another unsuspecting man. "Rolly looks like a largemouth bass. Rolly looks like a largemouth bass. Hey, Largemouth, you missed the bait." Rolly's face reddened like a ripe tomato. Johanna was a little disappointed he had missed his mark. Largemouth immediately became Rolly's nickname from then on until he moved to Minneapolis eight years later.

During the breaks in the music, Billy joined his young friends and explored the vast expanses of the new back yard. They ran races around the perimeter and threw the baseball around to each other. They could wind up and throw the ball as hard as they wanted and did not run out of room in this new yard. So much room.

Mary also explored with the five or six little girls in attendance. At the far back end of the lot they immediately found the two wells. Mary ran and found Aunt Edith. "Why are there two wells here, Aunt?"

"The old well was going dry last fall and so my husband Hans and son Emil dug a newer, deeper well over here. The old well was filled with all the dirt from the new well. You can play by the old well all you want but be very careful to not fall in the new one."

The girls circled around the old well several times. Some of the stones and bricks had come out of the walls. The grass was worn down here from all the feet that had stood there over the years. Mary's eyes lit up. "I will be right back." She ran to the new house, found her box of toy things and hauled several dolls down to the old well. "We can play house here," she announced to her friends. She placed Big Daddy Doll on the highest perch in a perfect space on the well wall. "Be careful, children, don't go near the new well by yourself,." warned Big Daddy Doll. What fun as the little friends jumped right in to the game.

At five o'clock Pastor Jorstad clapped his hands and used his booming preacher voice to get everyone's attention. First he led a cheer for Edith and her good Christian deed. The bombastic cheers bounced off the barn, ending in a "Hip, Hip, Hooray." He pulled out his Bible and church prayer book and prepared to give the new Stadler home a special blessing.

"I would like to ask us all to take a moment of silence and personal prayer for Charles Stadler. Charles was a great family man and would have been so appreciative of all this support for his wife and children. He would have reserved his biggest thanks for Edith who has become a sister and aunt to the Stadlers this winter." Pastor paused a moment. "Let us also remember Hans Hanson in our thoughts and prayers. He needs our spiritual help as much as anyone right now."

No one wanted to say anything after that. After a few minutes of silence, Pastor piped up, "Okay, now for the blessing of this new home for the Stadlers.

"We bless the use of this gift house as a place to raise an amazing family. Lord, make this home a place of peace. Bless the gardens out back for a bountiful harvest which will sustain both the Stadler family and their new Aunt Edith. Protect the new well in the back pasture so it may bring life-sustaining water for the livestock and the crops. Thank you Lord for the Christian neighborliness shown by this community all winter and today. May we all continue to grow as a Christian family, showing patience, mercy and concern for each other as we live out our God-given lives here in Minnesota. Amen."

Another round of "Hip, hip, Hoorays" sprang forth followed by a spontaneous singing of the new hymn *Will the Circle Be Unbroken*.

The crowd packed up and all headed next to Edith's new home The procession looked like one of the old pioneer wagon trains as it wormed it's way along the road, over the river bridge and out to the old Stadler place. The furniture and boxes were unpacked very swiftly. When all the movers had found their way out to the front yard, Pastor Jorstad raised his arms up, palms out, and calmed the people down to near silence. He led a new prayer for Edith's house followed by another singing of *Will the Circle Be Unbroken.*

After the neighbors left for home, and the Stadlers had returned to their new house, Billy ran up the stairs to the second floor. He found his new bed room. Mother had told him he could choose one of the biggest rooms since he would be sharing with little Charles as soon as the baby outgrew the cradle.

Mary sat down right in the middle of her room. She was not sharing with anyone. She had her own little room. Her huge eyes took in all the space around her. Her bed would fit over against the wall. Her dresser there next to the door and that wall under the window is perfect for her dolls and dollhouse. She fell asleep right there in the middle of the room and curled up on her special blanket.

Johanna marveled at the size of her bedroom. She could place a desk there at the end of the room to serve her as a private study. Mr. Johnson had promised to construct as large a bookshelf as he could for the wall. The city librarian would have hundreds of her own books, right?

Ellie was glad to claim the other smaller bedroom, a cozy spot on the corner of the house with windows on both walls for light and ventilation. And still there was room for her small rocking chair. Someone had tucked the cradle next to her headboard.

Once the Stadlers left and all the wonderful neighbors had gone home, Edith stood in the middle of the downstairs. This house was quite familiar to her but not with her own furniture in it. She felt at peace. She knew she had done the right thing to exchange homes with the Stadlers. She inspected the three bedrooms upstairs, the larger one for her (and Hans when he returned home?) and the others for small guest rooms. Maybe Emil would come home soon. She loved the configuration of the kitchen and pantry. She looked out the window. The barn was plenty large for her carriage and the horses. Ellie and the family were going to raise the other livestock over at the bigger house. Most satisfying of all was that the Stadlers were now set to succeed in the new larger place. Children need room to expand, room to jump and run outside and room to expand their minds inside. She sat down in her rocking chair. Life is good. I only wish that Hans, and dear Emil, were here now to share with me.

Chapter 41

Summer 1907

Life settled down into a routine quickly after the house exchange. Billy and Johanna finished their year at the country school. Billy passed on to the next grade, scoring in the middle of his class. His teacher was surprised when she saw the results--usually a student lost ground in school when something catastrophic happened during the year. She knew how much he missed his father but the responsibilities he was given by Johanna and his mother seemed to keep him focused. After the brief time when Billy had fought back against the bullying from Henry and his other friends, the young boy had transformed into a model student and citizen. Billy was even helping his friends with their math assignments, passing on the tips he learned from his sister. Miss Anders was looking forward to the next year in school. She felt that even at his young age, Billy would be a leader in the schoolhouse classroom and not in the schoolhouse doghouse. Billy was presented with the young citizen award for the lower grades. His faced beamed like the summer sun when she put the medal around his neck.

Johanna had blossomed before her teacher's eyes. Initially Jo had sunk deep into herself when she realized that her college dream was floating away. Miss Block had a chance to talk with her one afternoon when Billy had missed class due to an illness. Miss Block asked her to stay after class to review the student papers that Jo had helped correct. The conversation was soon steered to the future and Jo did not seem to have any misgivings about staying in Centerville after graduation. She asked her teacher if she was a church person and when Miss Block indicated that she attended the Congregational Church in town, Jo's face lit up.

"You know about the Apostle Paul then, right? He spoke about the idea that everyone on earth have gifts from the Spirit, not just the pastors. I have understood that my gift lies in teaching and encouragement to my neighbors here in Centerville. I can influence the young children in the schools and the adults in the Carnegie Library to be their best. I dream of these people as living and walking architectural plans. This is even more exciting than the idea of drawing engineering plans for inanimate buildings or roads."

Miss Block could see the vision that Johanna described. She reflected, "Jo can pull this off. Her spirit and drive is inexhaustible. I predict the name of Johanna Stadler will be known across the state in a few years."

Ellie kept plenty busy raising her family. The large house needed some getting used to. The extra space was quickly incorporated into the family flow. One extra room on the first floor became the family library and study room. This allowed the children to work on bigger projects because the material did not have to be put away before every meal. Another empty room became Ellie's sewing room. Ellie admitted that this room was the messiest in the house but what a luxury.

The older children were such good helpers, especially out in the larger garden and pastures that came with the house. Billy and Johanna designed a covered walkway that went from the barn to the other outbuildings. Johanna drew up the plans, using the principles of building design she had gleaned from her independent studying of the Carnegie library books. Billy supervised several neighbor men with the construction. The elders were so good at teaching Billy the skills that they had. Pastor Jorstad appeared often in these months and spent many precious hours with Billy. He had the same kind of patience with the youngster as Charles had possessed. Ellie knew that the two of them had discussed Charles' disappearance. Billy was much less angry about that day. Sheriff John also made it out to the farm regularly. He had purchased a ball glove himself and spent hours throwing the ball back and forth with Billy. One weekend in June Sheriff and Deputy Coffey took Billy and several of his friends way over to Minneapolis to see a real baseball exhibition game. Billy talked about that trip constantly for three weeks. Even Ellie knew most of the players on the Minnesota team by the end of the summer.

Mary adored little Charlie, always including him in her doll play. She thought that Charlie was her live doll. Ellie had to watch her little "mommy" real carefully to make sure Mary did not try to take Charlie outside with her other dolls. Mary was especially good at letting Ellie know when Baby Charlie had a mess in his pants. 'Hope this still goes when she is old enough to help change them, too,' Ellie laughed.

Anytime the weather was nice Mary would carry her dolls out to the back yard and play around the old filled-in well that the Hansons had abandoned last fall. She called it Daddy Doll's Fort. Three or four bricks were missing in the old walls. Her biggest doll, Big Daddy Doll, was always propped up on the highest hole near the top of the well wall. Then Mary would lower the pitch of her voice as much as possible and croak, "I will protect you all. I am the Daddy. I will not go away." She would grab Daddy Doll and give him a big hug. As she watched from the yard or garden, her mother knew that this play was good therapy for her little daughter. Mary was often more clinging in the evening after a day playing out back by the well. She still missed her father greatly.

At mid-summer Mary realized that autumn would bring her first year at school. She was ready. She would park herself at the kitchen table with a book and tablet and pretend to be her sister Johanna working on her studies. She started practicing printing her numbers and letters.

Billy often asked his friends over that summer to help with

the chores and the big garden in the back yard. The boys enjoyed exploring out in the far back of the lot, behind the two wells where the forest came up to the pasture land. One day Billy found an old, rusty pocket knife that looked like the same kind that his father had. It still worked well, especially after he took some steel wool to it to burnish the rust away. After working the garden a while, the boys would always end up playing catch with the baseball. Billy never missed the chance to tell his buddies about his baseball glove's history and the story of his Uncle William. One day during the play he declared to all his friends that he was going to change his name to William. No more Billy.

"I ain't Billy no more, I am William," he announced balancing on the wall of the old well.

Later on in the house he found his mother. "I have to change my name, Mother. From now on, I am William. I am growed up now. "

"Yes, you are, Billy. I mean--William. Yes, you are. You are all growed up."

The large, communal garden produced like never before. Ellie and Edith devoted many days to weeding and watering the vegetables. Ellie would put the large basket with Baby Charles under the shade oak tree. Charles would converse with the songbirds and wave back at the leaves on the branches over his head. He would smile so sweetly whenever his mother or Aunt

Edith appeared. He downright crowed in excitement when his sister Mary dipped her face in to say hello.

Life was lonely without her Charles, but Ellie had to say also that her life was good. Our family is strong. She could see parts of Charles in each of the children, parts of Charles that would continue to grow for many years. She remembered the special passage in Matthew she had found after Christmas. In the Bible it was Jesus talking but she also thought of Charles saying "I will be with you alway, even to the end of the earth."

Chapter 42

October 1907

What is this? Ellie pulled out an envelope from Mary's book bag. "Mrs. Stadler" was printed carefully on the outside. Miss Anders, the elementary teacher, had slipped it in. The letter was about Billy.

Overall Billy has done well in school. Last week, however, was an aberration. He picked a fight with each of his friends, one after another. Bloody nose for Henry, his best friend. Pressure applied, no harm done. The two were playing baseball again by the afternoon recess. His school work is down a bit too. Recently, several papers have been turned in incomplete. Can we meet soon?

Sincerely,
Miss Anders

Ellie saw the date at the top. October 15. The one year anniversary of Father Gone. Her uncried tears flowed down her cheeks. One year.

The next day, when her new neighbor had stopped to pick up her children, Ellie told him she wanted to take the children to school. The three neighbor children climbed in the Stadler carriage, their father excited to have a little more time today to work the fields. Billy did not venture a look at his mother; he knew he was in trouble.

A short mother-teacher conference in the office had Billy on edge. Mother came out red-eyed, slumped over at the shoulders. Ms. Anders came out with a smile and an encouraging pat on Mother's shoulder.

No further punishment followed that afternoon. At recess, Billy, usually the leader on the playground, let his friends pick the games for the day. Henry still picked baseball. Everything was back to normal.

That evening at supper, the whole family told stories about Father. Tears flowed aplenty but the sound of laughter won out.

Ellie and Johanna offered prayers for the family. A new play by Mary starring Big Daddy Doll capped off the entertainment.

Chapter 43

Over the years

Life in the northern plains was not like the surrounding flat terrain. It was more like a roller-coaster with ups and downs, peaks and valleys. The Stadler life-wagon rattled down the road, plodding along. No further catastrophes, no broken axle, no runaway team. Of course, the wheels stuck in the mud a couple times, buried to the axle with setbacks and challenges. In the Midwest, all families had their bumps and bruises. That was the typical life in Minnesota.

Each cycle of fall and winter the family contracted inward, huddling to keep warm and to feel the human contact. With each spring, the joy of renewal filled the hearts of everyone. That was the life cycle of Midwest living.

The Stadler family spoke often of Charles. No new theories emerged about his disappearance. Many of the family believed he had fallen into the river. Johanna was spooked whenever someone mentioned the Peat Bog. Ellie and the children did not believe that their loving husband and father could have walked off into a new life, leaving them to survive on their own. The spirit of Charles was there in the family love and courage, in the fortitude and adjustments they all had to make over the following years.

The town of Centerville grew and grew, centered on the burgeoning railroad line. As the years went by, the surrounding country roads improved and trips to town became easier. The rural schools both west of town and east, closed and Billy and Mary rode into town to school with Johanna each morning as she continued on to the Carnegie library. After school they would walk over to the city library where they did their lessons until Jo was done. Billy loved to shelve the return books for Jo. The bulletin board above Jo's private desk was filled with Mary's stick-figure drawings of the family and the animals. Father was in each picture, towering protectively over the others.

Year after year other Centerville families would deal with losses and tragedies. The Great War saw many of the young men disappear as they fled off to Europe or Canada to sign up for their armies. Billy was tempted to follow; tempted to lie about his age and sign up for the army. But, in the end, he reasoned that he had a family to protect. He was the man in the Stadler family. The American draft ended the year he was nineteen, before he could be conscripted into the army. He was never called to service.

As the city librarian, Johanna became entrenched in the workings of the town. The library traffic increased each year. The building committee gave some token opposition to

Johanna's plans for expansion, especially the very niece that had introduced Andrew Carnegie to the small town, but in 1917 a large library addition was begun.

Johanna eventually decided to try a new occupation and moved over to the newly-formed Minnesota Reform School for Girls as the math teacher and librarian. This school was built by the state right there in Centerville since the railroad transportation was so convenient. At the school Johanna Stadler thrived in her role of educator and role model. She was too busy to take notice of the many young men who took notice in her. Eventually she passed the library off to a younger teacher and assumed the role of counselor. Most of the girls enrolled here had experienced tough knocks in their family and they connected immediately with Miss Stadler. Johanna recited the story of her family often.

Sinclair Lewis' novel *Main Street* appeared on the scene in 1925. Arguments burst out around his scandalous portrayal of small town Midwest life. This novel was not a positive picture of the Midwest townspeople. In his novel, most of the native Minnesotans were stuck in the past and resisted change. Lewis was from Sauk Centre but he persistently claimed the Main Street in his book was a generic place. He insisted that it was not about Sauk Centre. Behind the scenes, the novel sold very well in Sauk Centre, and neighboring Centerville, and all the little towns in Minnesota.

The story of Charles disappearance stayed with the Stadler family even as the generations grew up and began to spread out from the home town. Each Christmas a time of reflection was included at each family dinner prayer time. With each generation the personal nature of the story faded a bit more until the story became a legend, The Legend of Charles Stadler. No new clues presented themselves regarding that day in October 1906. Speculations were argued each family reunion, back and forth, over and over. Charles sank in the quicksand field. Charles fell into the river. Some even said, Charles ran away to seek his fortune in Alaska.

The fortitude of the family was the real marvel at these reunions. How Ellie had held the family together that first year. How Edith came like an angel to rescue the family, offering her friendship and trading homes. How Johanna gave up her dreams of being an engineer. How Billy grew up to be a star baseball player, first in high school and then in college. Each family reunion the stories would flow around the group. The mothers and grandmothers would gather the children together to make sure they heard these stories. The strength of the family became the true legend.

Then......78 years later, yes, two generations later, Charles' granddaughter Louise received a pleasant surprise, a letter from Tom, an old schoolmate from Centerville. The letter started out cordially, wondering how Louise was doing. (It had been over forty years since Louise and Tom had graduated from Centerville High.) Then, imagine this, the letter continued on to the subject of Louise' grandfather. Tom recalled that Louise was the oldest daughter of William (Billy) Stadler, thus making her the grand-daughter of Charles. What was this? Louise thought. She read that Tom had been at the bedside of his ancient Great Uncle Emil Hanson and had heard, of all things, Emil's deathbed confession. The mystery of Charles Stadler was solved; a massive yoke was lifted from her shoulders just as a ton of bricks hit her in the head. Now she knew the true details of that horrible day in October 1906. Now she could share with her daughters and her sister and nieces. Now the story of Charles Stadler was complete.

Louise and her family debated whether to go over to the nursing home in Minneapolis to show their Great Aunt Johanna. She was the only survivor from the 1906 Stadlers. Would this be too much of a strain on the 94 year old? Would she even understand what this letter said? Would she want to know the truth? In the end they decided that, yes, Johanna needed to know the story.

Do you want to know? Are you ready?

O.K. The rest of the story of October 1906…

Part Two

Chapter 44

October 15, 1906

.... Charles was back to the mail office early. No sign of Ralph. He must still be out on the east side rural and city route. He unhooked the carriage from Old Grey and put her in her stall with an extra big supper of corn and hay. As he entered the back door, he noticed a brown package on the counter.

"What is this? I must have put this piece in Ralph's pile when I sorted this morning. Who is it for? Oh, the Hansons. That's no problem. I can drop it off on my way home. The path runs through the woods only about a quarter mile away from their back lot. Boy, I'm getting hungry."

Charles was still excited that he would get home early that day. Running this small parcel over to the Hanson farm wouldn't cost him but a couple minutes. With the small package under his arm, he sprinted out of town. The make-shift path was still wet and slippery in some shaded places. He picked up three large branches that he had jumped over in the morning and threw them over into the woods out of the way. "When we get a little snow later this fall those branches will be much more dangerous, hiding under the white snow. Guaranteed to trip an unsuspecting walker. "

About one mile out of town he began to hear the men at the Hanson house. He could tell they were still feverishly working on the new well. A chaotic collection of grunts, shouts, and curses mixed with the clang of a shovel fighting with a bucket told him that. "Hope the well project is going better than it sounds from here." Charles turned off the path and picked his way through the underbrush and trees toward the sounds.

Breaking through the forest edge, Charles could see the high pile of dirt next to the new well hole. Hans was standing at the edge of the hole, partially hidden by the pile. He had his hands on a muddy rope coming out of the well.

A ladder was perched inside of the hole, only the top three rungs showing. A burst of louder shouting and cursing raged over to Charles. The younger Hanson, Emil, emerged from the hole, covered in black dirt and mud. As Charles approached he could hear everything clearly.

"Where are you going, you worthless piece of crap. Get back down there! We need to finish this today." There was no mistaking the booming, angry voice of the elder Hanson.

"I need a break and I need to take a piss. You want me to piss right there in the well, do you?"

Emil threw his red stocking cap out of the well opening,

followed shortly by his tall, thin six foot body. He started to walk over to the back side of the old well fumbling with his button fly. Hans jumped around the hole right after his son, screaming at the top of his lungs. He tripped over a shovel on the ground, almost going down.

Hans grabbed the shovel as he caught his balance with his out-stretched arm. He rushed at his son, the shovel trailing behind him on the ground. "You are a worthless piece of crap. Just as worthless as your older brother who disappeared to Alaska. I will tell you when we take a break."

The son turned around to face his father. Strings of curse words jumped into the air between them. Emil braced himself to run at his father, to knock him down.

Charles could see only trouble coming from this encounter. He rushed up the widening path, turned into the yard, dropped the package next to the old well and ran to get between the two men. He put his arms high over his head and hugged Emil, trying to push him away from the father. "All right, you guys. Just cool it here. You won't get the well done with this fighting. Just take five minutes to simmer down."

But Hans didn't stop. His rage had built up over the last three days and was boiling over out of control. He continued to yell at his son, "I don't want to hear any of your shit anymore." He stared at the son's head and shoulders. He didn't even register that Charles was there. All he could see was his white rage. The shovel came up impulsively and slashed through the air at his son. The shovel blade sliced into the back of Charles' head and neck with a loud thud. Blood spurted everywhere. Charles slumped toward the ground like a wet noodle, sliding down Emil's chest. He ended up crumpled in a disorganized pile at Emil's feet.

Hans and Emil stared at Charles in shock. Then both well-diggers yelled out at the same time, "Oh, my God, Oh, my God."

Hans fell to the ground, staring at the body one shovel length in front of him. His son knelt down and quickly turned Charles' body over. Charles' eyes were wide open, frozen in the terror he felt that last second of his life. Emil torn open Charles' jacket, looked at his chest. No chest movement, no breath out of his mouth. No life left in this lump of human. "Oh, my God. What have we done? What have we done?"

Chapter 45

Hans scurried over on hands and knees to Charles' body, sticky blood mixed with dirt clinging to his hands. He shook them disgustingly trying to clean off the death slurry. He jumped up and ran over to the pile of fresh dirt, scratching his gnarled hands in the moist soil to rub off the filthy muck. Only then did he look over at Charles and Emil.

"You big lout. Why didn't you tell me Charles was there? Why did you let me hit him? "

Emil cowered away from his father. His words were trapped behind his tongue.

"I ...I... didn't....he just appeared....too late."

"Well help him up. Get him to his feet."

Emil looked squarely at his father's face. "Dad, he is dead. You killed him, Dad. He is dead. Charles is gone. "

Hans looked more closely at the body. He saw no movement, no life. He jumped over again to the corpse to confirm this reality. He shook the body several times. Finally he dropped his neighbor to the ground. He reached into Charles' pockets and found only Charles' large pocket knife and a couple coins.

Emil's voice woke him up to the real world again. "We need to tell someone in town quick, Dad. We need to call Sheriff Braun. Tell him how it was an accident. You didn't know Charles was there. He sprang up from out of nowhere, Dad. I didn't know he was on my chest. You didn't know either. We need to tell the sheriff."

Brandishing Charles' small blade and waving it in his son's face, Hans hissed, "Shut up. Are you crazy? I can't go whimpering up to that Braun guy. He hates me. We have history. He caught me robbing the tavern years ago and has never given me a second chance since. He hates me......We ain't telling no one. Just you and me, Emil. Not even your mother. Remember that. Just you and me."

He looked threateningly at his son. He spoke slowly so Emil could digest each and every word. Hans grabbed Emil's face with his free hand and stared straight into his eyes. "Now that I got blood on my hands, I'll come for you next if any of this leaks out. You hear me. I'm serious. Anything leaks and......" He sliced the blade in front of Emil's neck.

The knife blade caught the sunlight and flashed a vicious signal. Hans glanced down at the weapon, realized it had belonged to Charles, and threw it off into the long grass away from the wells.

Emil looked in his father's eyes. He had suffered the abuse of his father for all his years. He knew that his father would be true to his word. His father's eyes were glazed over; pupils wide open in terror, staring holes in Emil's face. Emil knew that he could never tell a soul.

"But what about the body? What do we say about the body? It is just lying there in the dirt."

"We get rid of the evidence, you useless dunce. Help me-- now."

The corpse was difficult to move, all that dead weight, all that blood. At first, the two men grabbed and pulled, each in his own direction. Finally Hans barked out the orders and Charles was folded up and carried over to the wall of the old dry well, lifted over the top and dropped down the hole. A small splash and thud announced its arrival in the muck at the bottom. Only then did Hans notice the package that Charles had dropped as he ran to Emil. Hans tore it open. It was one of those fancy dresses Edith had ordered by mail. A Big blot of blood covered the outside of the package and now it stained the dress too. He threw the package and dress into the well on top of the body.

"She will never miss this one package. We never saw it, right? And throw that outer shirt of yours in, it's covered in Stadler's blood.

Shovel by shovel, they furiously covered up the evidence. The bloodiest dirt was thrown in first. Eventually the dirt filled up the well to the top of the wall. Only when the dirt pile heaped over the top did they stop and rest. Hans ordered Emil to climb up on the soil and stamp it down. Hans collapsed on the ground next to the new well and covered his face in shame. Emil ran off into the woods and sat with his back against a giant oak tree, facing away from the mess, and wept.

The sun began to sink behind the forest. The largest oak tree shadowed the death scene. Eventually they got back to work on the new well. Somehow they found the focus necessary to push the corpse into the back of their minds. The men had previously piled a selection of flatter stones to line the new well. Only the last three feet of the hole still needed stones. They busied themselves with this final task. The underground spring in the bottom of the new well that they had reached earlier that afternoon was already slowly, efficiently filling the new pit with fresh water. As the last light faded out in the horizon the last stone found its place. The men gathered up the shovels and picks and followed their noses along the familiar path to the house. Hans glowered at Emil as they jumped up on the porch, shaking his fist threateningly. Lastly, he brandished his long finger, slashing it in the air in front of Emil's neck.

Supper was warmed up for the two men. Edith knew they were exhausted. She hadn't been able to see the flurry of work way back there by the wells but she knew that they must have put in extra work to finish by dark. In spite of the huge job the men had done they barely had an appetite that night. Edith couldn't get them interested in her cooking, not even the pies she had baked specially for them.

"They must be totally exhausted," Edith thought.

Emil excused himself first and went upstairs to wash and then to bed. Hans walked over directly to the cabinet by the fireplace and pulled out the dusty whiskey bottle from the back of the shelf. He hadn't touched that bottle in four years. Edith had been too afraid to throw it away when she would find it while cleaning. She had hoped Hans had forgotten where that bottle was. Edith whole body shook as she watched him swallowing the hard liquor right from the bottle neck.

"Oh, my dear Lord, please keep that trouble away from us now. He has been doing so well. Oh Lord, please."

Chapter 46

Hans had not stopped drinking two hours later when Edith went up to bed. She heard his bass snoring out on the couch shortly after she lay down. Lying in bed, looking up at the ceiling, Edith thought about the tough days she had endured early in their marriage when Hans drank every night. The arrival of the two boys had sobered Hans up then. Each time he took up the bottle again she managed to appeal to his pride as a father. What kind of role model do you want to be? She would plead with him. The last time, when Hans Junior had fled the farm, Edith and Hans both knew that if he ever started again, even one drink, his life would crash again. She slept restlessly in their bed.

Hans was still sleeping in his chair when Edith awoke with the roosters. The east horizon was brightening, no clouds in the sky today. Edith let Hans sleep. "There was no sense stirring him up now. He would not be worth anything out in the fields today, at least until noon. The new well had been finished last night. Let him sleep. I pray that he wakes with a bucket load of remorse."

Emil woke shortly after she did. He went into the washroom and splashed his face awake. When he came down for breakfast he was silent. His head was down, he shuffled across the floor.

"Want some pancakes and eggs and ham, son?"

He barely nodded his head.

"He must still be tired from yesterday," Edith thought.

Emil went out to the barn after breakfast and fed the animals. He cleaned the stalls thoroughly. He did not go anywhere near the wells.

After the chores were done Emil took up the scythe and headed out to the hayfields to whack down the hay. He worked right through lunch and came in silently at dusk, shuffled to the table again, ate quietly and went upstairs without a word to his mother.

Hans woke up about three in the afternoon, went upstairs to change clothes, and headed straight out to take the carriage into town.

"When will you be home, dear?"

"Don't have a clue. Can't a man go to town without being nagged to death? "

Edith sat at the fire alone that evening. Something must have happened out at the new well last night. Emil is always trying to defend his older brother. They must have gotten into a big row about Hans Junior. Bringing up that name would surely put Hans into a state. Just hope they crawl out of this dark cloud before too long.

But neither man showed any signs of getting back to normal. All week the family lived separate lives, Hans at the tavern in town, Emil out in the fields and Edith in her home all alone.

Chapter 47

Early November, 1906

Emil had finished the cutting of the hay and the warm autumn weather and sun had dried it out. The crop was ready for gathering. That was a two man job.

After breakfast Emil hung around out in the barnyard until his father came out to get the team ready for town. "Father, we need to get the hay up in the loft, I can't do that alone."

"Of course you can't do that alone. I ain't stupid. Let's get to it right now." He shifted a bottle from the carriage seat to the pocket of his jacket. He disconnected the team from the carriage and hitched them to the large hay wagon. Silently they rode out to the field.

Amazingly, once the two of them started in on the task at hand, they worked as if they were two pistons of the same engine. Emil threw the hay up unto the wagon bed and Hans moved it into a compact pile in the front. In three hours they had completed the first load, brought it into the yard, stopped at the house for a quick lunch and headed back out to the field. Twice more they loaded the wagon. The sun was disappearing over the horizon as they climbed on one last time to come home.

"Father, I cannot live like this. I see Charles Stadler's face and all that blood in front of me all day long every day. We need to go to the sheriff and tell the truth. It was an accident, father. He will understand that we panicked and hid him in the well. That is just human nature. Anyone would do that."

Hans glared at his son.

"I told you we will never talk about that again. That piece-of-shit sheriff will never believe me if I confess. You don't know how much he hates me. I will tell you this one more time--never again. If you ever say a word about that day I will not hesitate to kill you on the spot. You are just as useless as that brother of yours. Ever since he left us here on the farm, I have known him for what he is---- a nothing. How dare he think he can escape this hole of a place ahead of me? And I know you have kept in contact with him somehow. I know you know where he is. Run to him. You deserve each other. Two piles of crap make one big stink."

The ride into the farm was deafeningly quiet. Emil did not look at his father again. After the unloading of the hay and another silent supper, Emil went up to his room.

When the next morning came, Emil was late to come down for breakfast. Finally, Edith went upstairs and knocked on his door. She heard nothing. She pushed open the door a crack and looked in on the bed. The covers were pulled back, the bed was empty. She went in slowly. The drawers were wide open and empty. Emil's valise was gone. He had sneaked out in the night.

On the dresser was a sheet of paper with one sentence scrawled across it

I love you, Mother.

Your son, Emil

Chapter 48

The next months

Miraculously, Hans never said a word about his crime. Liquor did not loosen up his tongue. He kept to himself at the taverns and the other men knew enough to leave him alone. Don't mess with him. Hans was just another lonely, troubled old man, drowning his problems in his whiskey.

Edith could not understand what happened to Hans. She did know deep in her heart that he was lost to her-- he was never coming back this time. Secretly, she hoped that her two sons had somehow found each other. Maybe in a few years they would learn that their father had drunk himself dead and they would come home. Luckily, she had found the Stadlers. That was a real blessing. She felt so good about her new little house. The big Stadler house was so alive with the noises of that wonderful family. Ellie was raising an incredible collection of people. Johanna will never get her math degree but she was so proud of the town library and her first accomplishments with the school library. Billy was such a responsible young man; one forgets he was only nine years old now. I think he will turn out just fine. Mary was following the other two in school. At home she had such imagination, always play-acting with her dolls. And she was a little mother to Baby Charlie. Mary loved to play out by the old well with Big Daddy Doll.. She was so cute. She was always saying that her Father was not gone; he was with them each day. She would point to her heart and would recite:

Father is right here,
He is always very near.

Thank you, first and foremost, to my lovely wife. She shared the remarkable true story from her family which forms the backbone of this fictional work.

Thank you to my readers, Sue, Kay, Anne, Lisa and Grace, who plodded through my first two drafts and provided such valuable feedback. Of course, all errors in spelling, grammar, and structure are solely mine as the only editor.

Thank you also to my friends of the Chippewa Falls Library writers group who has given me such confidence and support.